About t

After an inauspicious five years at the Guernsey Grammar School for Boys, when greater effort was paid to larking about than to academic study, I somehow attained four O-levels, including English Language and English Literature. I had hoped to stay on for A-level English, but the headmaster informed my parents that to do so would be a complete waste of everybody's time!

Hence, a thirty-year career with the Guernsey Civil Service and then, once my children had left school and the mortgage cleared, a decision to revisit my affection for English with three years as a reporter with the Guernsey Press and nine years in public relations.

All of this has led to the blissful state that is retirement, affording me the time and de-cluttering of mind to write this book. I hope it provides some enjoyment for a few people as we make our way through these modern times.

A BREED APART

Neil Robin

A BREED APART

Vanguard Press

A CIP catalogue record for this title is
available from the British Library.

ISBN 978-1-80016-428-4

Vanguard Press is an imprint of
Pegasus Elliot Mackenzie Publishers Ltd.
www.pegasuspublishers.com

First Published in 2022

Vanguard Press
Sheraton House Castle Park
Cambridge England

Printed & Bound in Great Britain

Dedication

This book is dedicated to my wife and family and the small band of good friends who have all stuck with me for many years, when the easier option may well have been to bail out! It is also dedicated to the island of Guernsey, from where, observing the difficulties affecting much of the outside world, we cannot take for granted how fortunate we are to live in such a delightful and safe environment.

Prologue

This book is based on events in the life of the author's grandfather, Ted Robin, from just before the onset of World War One until just after the end of World War Two.

Ted was born and raised in Guernsey. For those perhaps not too familiar with the island, the outline below gives a flavour of its geography and history.

Guernsey is one of the Channel Islands — along with Jersey, Alderney, Sark and Herm — which form an archipelago situated in the English Channel, lying in the shelter of the Bay of St Malo.

Although the islands switched allegiance from the French Crown to the English Crown in the year 1204, their geographical position (less than fifteen miles from the French coast, but more than seventy miles from the English coast) has meant that they have retained a strong connection to their roots, with many families, places and roads bearing French names.

As the western-most of the islands and lying in the path of the Gulf Stream, Guernsey is blessed with a mild climate, ideal for the cultivation of crops such as tomatoes and freesias.

Although only nine miles long by five miles wide, the island had hundreds of glasshouses in the early part of the twentieth century, with good sea links to markets in southern England providing the main export outlet for its crops.

Horticulture, therefore, provided the main source of employment for most of Guernsey's working population, while the island's dairy herd produced a rich, creamy milk that was hugely popular in the English markets and a carefully-managed trade of livestock saw a small quota of Guernsey cows and bulls being exported to the UK, and some then onward across the Atlantic to America.

Chapter 1

It was against the backdrop of growing unrest in mainland Europe in the early part of 1914 that the people of the island of Guernsey went about their daily lives.

Ted Robin was twenty years of age and worked in his father's joinery business, which was quite a busy venture given the afore-mentioned proliferation of wooden-framed glasshouses covering much of the island at that time.

His parents, Nicholas and Elizabeth Robin, had three sons and the eldest, Edwin (or Ted as he was known to everyone except his father), had finished school at the age of fourteen in order to learn the joinery trade under the stern tuition of his father.

The proudest moment in Ted's life, to that point, and in fact the only time that he felt that his father was ever really proud of him, was when Nicholas changed the sign above the workshop door from *"N. Robin — Master Joiner"* to *"N. Robin & Son — Master Joiners"*.

At six feet in height, Ted was surprisingly tall, given that both of his parents were a good six inches shorter, and a strong physique enabled him to lift and carry items into and out of the workshop, something his aging father now found difficult to manage. However, despite his stature, Ted was not a particularly outgoing type and this was possibly as a result of his father's domineering style.

The middle son, William (or Billy, as the rest of the family called him when Nicholas was not within earshot), was seventeen years of age and while he was not blessed with the same physical build as his older brother, he was rather more of a scholar than Ted. After staying on at school for an extra couple of years, Billy had recently embarked on a career as a trainee reporter with the island's newspaper, the Guernsey Evening Press.

The youngest son, Charles (Charlie), was just fifteen and, like Ted, had been keen to leave school as soon as possible to learn a trade. He, too, was not particularly tall, but was solidly built and had recently been taken on at the bicycle sales and repair shop owned by their uncle, Alfred Robins.

The family lived in a modest house on the outskirts of Guernsey's main town, St Peter Port, with Nicholas's workshop attached to the side of the house. A typical Guernsey house of the time, it comprised of a living room and kitchen downstairs, outside toilet and two bedrooms upstairs, one of which was shared by the three brothers.

There was one more member of the household, namely Elizabeth's much younger sister, Edith Breton, who was eighteen years of age. Edith slept in a small lean-to shed abutting the outside toilet, which Nicholas had built when she came to live with them a couple of years earlier.

Elizabeth's parents had long accepted that they were destined to have just one child and so it came as a complete surprise to them when her mother fell pregnant again in her mid-forties, when Elizabeth was twenty-two and married with a two-year-old son of her own.

Tragically though, Elizabeth's mother died in childbirth and it fell to Mr Breton to raise their daughter through her formative years. The difficult birth may also have been the reason that Edith was quite a sickly child. She missed a good deal of her school years through being confined to bed with various illnesses.

Elizabeth did her best to visit her father and sister as often as possible to help with laundry and cooking and nursing Edith when she was poorly, but the fact that it was a four-mile walk from her house to theirs and then another four miles to walk back home again, combined with raising her own family, meant that this could not happen as often as they all might like.

However, Elizabeth was an accomplished, self-taught seamstress and began a business mending garments for people in the neighbourhood. When Edith reached school-leaving age, Elizabeth suggested to her father that Edith should move to live with her and learn the skill of sewing.

While he was disappointed to lose the company of his younger daughter, Mr Breton was also quietly relieved to pass on the stewardship of a somewhat headstrong teenage girl. He knew that living with her older sister would better prepare Edith for adult life.

Edith was elated to learn that she would be living with the Robin family, but mainly because she had held a special affection for Ted ever since they were small children and she secretly yearned for them to become even closer.

Uncle Alfred's house and bicycle shop were just a couple of doors away from Nicholas and Elizabeth's house and it was identical to theirs, except that the ground floor had been converted to accommodate the bicycle-repair business and Alfred lived in a two-roomed flat above.

The two brothers' properties were separated by a small cottage between them, which was the home of their elderly parents. Originally the cottage had stood detached with fields either side and behind, which their father had farmed in his younger days.

When Nicholas and, Alfred reached adulthood, they toiled long and hard to build themselves a house each, attached to each side of the cottage, with a small garden in front of each of the three dwellings and a large field running across the rear of them.

Although sporting a magnificent Santa-like, white beard, Nicholas was not a very cheerful character and ran his household according to strict principles emanating from his devout religious beliefs. While he may have been shorter than all three of his sons, he was as strong as an ox and quite capable of delivering severe corporal punishment when any of them stepped out of line.

While Ted and the other boys shared their father's Christian faith, they resented their firm upbringing by him and were also sad that their mother was largely unsuccessful in trying to intervene when he was being violent towards any of them.

The boys preferred their Uncle Alf, who was always teasing them, playing pranks and keen to play cricket or football with them in the field. Alfred, at forty years of age, was a decade younger than Nicholas and had never married, perhaps largely due to him taking on the responsibility of being the main carer for their elderly parents.

One aspect of his brother's life of which Nicholas strongly disapproved was Alfred's penchant for frequenting The Beehive, a public house on the corner of the road where they lived. He frequently warned his sons that their lives would not be worth living if he found out that any of them had been tempted by alcohol.

Nicholas was a keen member of the congregation of St Stephen's church, which stood at the other end of their road, and insisted on his family joining him at services there twice on Sundays and bible-reading classes on Thursday evenings.

Alfred, to the great disappointment of his brother, was not a church-goer and instead spent much of his Sundays with his parents and most evenings in The Beehive.

Elizabeth was the glue that held the whole family together, devotedly tending house and cooking and washing for them and vainly trying to be the peacemaker when any of the sons, or indeed Alfred or Edith, said or did anything that riled Nicholas.

In addition to Guernsey's geographical position dictating the island's economy, it also meant long, warm summers which provided the islanders with delightful evenings in which to enjoy their leisure time. This was something that Ted embraced as much as possible.

After long, hot days in the workshop, his routine was to rush through the obligatory ritual of the family evening meal and then to jump on his bicycle and pedal the two miles down the long hill from his house to Cobo Bay.

This long, sandy beach on the island's west coast was where Ted would meet the two most important people in his life after his own family; namely, his friends Dick Birdsall and Ruth Meunier.

Edith regularly asked if she could come to Cobo Bay with Ted, but he just wanted to get away from the family environment for a couple of hours and so he was quietly pleased that Edith did not have a bicycle with which to accompany him.

Ted and Dick had been best friends since they met in infants' school and, as an only child, Dick had always valued Ted like a brother.

Dick's father owned a fleet of horses and carts and his business was collecting the boxes of tomatoes and freesias from glasshouses around the island and delivering them to St Sampson's harbour, where they would be loaded onto ships and transported to the markets of southern England.

As was normal for most first-born sons in Guernsey at that time, Dick, like Ted, had left school at an early age to work in his father's business.

As he worked outdoors, driving a horse and cart every day, Dick sported a bronzed skin and frequently teased Ted for his very white skin, the result of being stuck indoors in the joinery workshop for eight hours every day.

Making up the trio of firm friends was Ruth Meunier, whose father owned a building company and, being more academically-inclined, Ruth had become the firm's book-keeper. Like Ted though, Ruth spent most of her days indoors and so she, too, was subjected to Dick's teasing for having a pale complexion.

"Ah, here come the two ghosts," Dick would often say, as Ted and Ruth lay their bicycles in the dunes and made their way down to join him on the beach.

The three of them would enjoy swimming, throwing pebbles in the sea, chatting happily for a couple of hours and watching the stunning sunsets, before Ted had to make the slog of a cycle ride back up the hill to get home.

"It's all right for you two living so close to the beach," he would moan to Dick and Ruth. "I've got to pedal up that blinking hill again."

"Ah, but think how much stronger your legs are than ours," Dick would tease. "We'd really love to be getting all that exercise every day."

While Dick was very fond of Ruth, it was clear that she leaned more towards Ted and he resigned himself to the fact that they would one day becoming a courting couple. Nicholas was certainly keen that his eldest son should settle down with her.

"Haven't you proposed to that Meunier girl yet, Edwin?" he often said. "You want to get a move on or she'll go off with that Birdsall lad instead."

"Leave the boy alone," Elizabeth would chide her husband. "You were twenty-five years old when you married me, so don't nag Edwin to do it any earlier."

Ted suspected that his father's motives had far more to do with the fact that Ruth came from a relatively wealthy family, rather than any great desire to see his son embark on married bliss!

Talk of Ted marrying someone else was a source of secret dismay to Edith, though. Despite being his aunt and Ted never showing anything other than platonic affection for her, she felt that she loved him dearly and she often dreamed that they might one day elope and live happily ever after.

Chapter 2

One of the perks of working for the Guernsey Evening Press was that every member of staff was permitted to take home a free copy of the newspaper each day and while William did so, Nicholas soon introduced the rule that he was always the first to read it.

One day in July 1914, the island's newspaper carried a lead story which was to herald the beginning of great division and resentment between Edwin and Nicholas and an animosity which would blight their relationship for the rest of their lives.

"They're going on about the Germans flexing their muscles in Europe again," Nicholas announced to his family. "Their army is bigger and better than anyone else's and it is feared that they will invade their neighbours very soon."

This news was being absorbed by many people in Guernsey and speculation began to spread about how the peaceful tranquillity of the little island might be affected.

Nicholas shared the widely held view that Guernsey men should play their part if the call came to confront the German advance and there was growing talk within the island of forming a Guernsey Militia to place at the disposal of the King.

"Guernsey didn't let the French push us around seven hundred years ago and we won't let the Germans do it now," Nicholas said. "All you young men can go and show them who's boss." To his great annoyance though, his eldest son did not share his views.

"I can't understand why countries want to steal each other's land and kill each other in the process," Ted said. "Why can't they all just live peacefully in their own space, like we do here?"

"Decent Christian countries do," retorted Nicholas, clearly putting aside the spread of the British Empire in days gone by. "But the devil has wormed his way into the minds of some other countries and it is our duty to fight them and him too."

"But we are taught in the Bible that thou shalt not kill," Ted reasoned. "How can it be God's will to do that?"

"I will not have the name of God used to justify cowardice," Nicholas thundered. "God has sanctioned setting aside his rules when the forces of the devil have challenged all that is right and good."

In an attempt to earn favour with his father, William decided to join the debate. "Well, I would relish the chance to join the Guernsey Militia as a war correspondent and go with them into Europe and send back reports," he said.

Also spotting an opportunity to gain his father's approval, Charles spoke up, too. "I'm not bothered about writing about it, I just want to get over there and fight for my King and my island," he said.

"There! That's the sort of spirit we should be showing," Nicholas smiled, triumphantly. "You see, Edwin, your younger brothers can teach you a thing or two."

It was with this heated exchange troubling his mind that Ted cycled off to meet his friends at the beach. He brooded on it throughout the ride to Cobo Bay and wasted no time in briefing Dick and Ruth about it when he joined them.

"My father has been bashing on about it, too, but he doesn't want me to go," Dick said. "I would happily volunteer, but he says that our business is providing a vital service here and so I can't be spared to go off for months on end."

"Well, I would love to join up, but we women aren't even allowed to vote, let alone fight," said Ruth, with some frustration. "We just have to stay at home and mind the house and children while the men go off and have all the fun."

As Ted was clearly getting no support from his friends for his view that conflict was the wrong way to go about settling disputes, he took early leave of them and cycled home feeling very lonely and apparently at odds with everyone that he held dear.

Only a few days later, news came through that the heir to the Austrian throne had been assassinated at Sarajevo, precipitating the outbreak of war in Europe. Then, over the ensuing weeks and months, reports appeared regularly in the Guernsey Press charting the advance of German forces through Belgium and into northern France.

British troops were deployed to the Somme to dig-in and effectively form a barricade to prevent the German advance progressing any further south. The Royal Guernsey Militia was duly formed, with an undertaking coming from the British Government to provide them with uniforms, weapons and training.

A contingent of British army personnel was due to arrive in the island shortly to deliver training in the art of trench warfare, following which the men of the Royal Guernsey Militia would be deployed to Northern France within weeks.

While these developments prompted concern among the Guernsey population in general, it was particularly the case for the chairman of the Guernsey Agriculture Council. He called an emergency meeting, accordingly.

Guernsey's prize asset was its unique cattle herd, which had been created centuries earlier by cross breeding prime French beef stock with prime English dairy stock. This had enabled the island to produce a breed capable of providing the sweetest and creamiest milk and the most tender and tasty beef.

This was something that generations of islanders had fiercely protected from outside influence and they had only grudgingly accepted the lucrative trade of exporting livestock in the late 1800s, when Guernsey's economy required a boost to finance the industrial revolution that was reaching its shores. A limited number of cattle were sent from the island every couple of years to farmers in the UK and America.

The Chairman of the Guernsey Agriculture Council (GAC) addressed the meeting.

"Gentlemen, we are faced with a most difficult decision. If the British line at the Somme should be broken, then the German Army will be less than fifty miles away from our shores. If they were to invade us, then our breed may be shipped away and cross-bred and then its purity will be lost forever."

A murmur of concern swept around the table as the gravity of the situation dawned on the other members there.

"Although we are not due to export any cattle this year, I propose that we evacuate a proportion of our herd," the Chairman continued. "I would suggest sixteen cows and four bulls be sent to a place of safety and we can recall them to the island when and if it is safe to do so."

"Are you suggesting that we send them to England, Mr Chairman?" asked another member.

"No, I am not, because I fear that the Hun could take that small step from Calais to Dover and then our herd would be no safer there than if it had stayed in Guernsey," the Chairman replied. "However, we have previously sent some of our livestock to a cattle association in Pennsylvania in the United States of America and I am proposing that we should send these twenty cattle there again now. My contact there assures me they would continue to honour the pledge not to cross breed from the Guernsey stock and so our cattle, or their descendants if this accursed war should drag on, would return to us with full purity and integrity intact."

The meeting duly ratified the Chairman's proposal and moved on to discuss the necessary arrangements to evacuate twenty cattle to America. It was noted that while a number of Guernsey men had accompanied the exported livestock in previous years, most of them were now committed to travelling to France with the Guernsey Militia to join the war effort.

It was, therefore, agreed that new personnel would need to be recruited for this particular trip and an advertisement was drawn up for submission to the Guernsey Evening Press.

Two days later, William arrived home with his free copy of the newspaper and the family listened as Nicholas read aloud the latest news on the war in France and then also the GAC advertisement that appeared on the front page.

"Five young men are required to escort Guernsey cattle to safety in America, for which a small remuneration will be paid. Those interested should report to the Guernsey Agriculture Committee offices at 6.30p.m. tomorrow evening."

The possibility of enemy forces invading their peaceful little island was one that had perhaps not fully impacted on some of the islanders. They knew that a battle was raging nearby in France, of course, and that many of the island's young men might get the chance to go to take part in the fighting there, but the realisation began to dawn that everyday life within the island itself could change forever if it should be occupied by a foreign force.

However, the advert in the Guernsey Evening Press about the evacuation of cattle to the United States of America filled the head of Edwin Robin with very different thoughts to those of his father and his brothers and many other Guernsey folk.

Retaining his strong conviction that war was wrong and there was no excuse for participating therein, Ted reasoned that if he could get on the trip to America it would, at least, delay the possibility of him being bullied into joining the Royal Guernsey Militia and going off to war.

He thought that perhaps the war might be over by the time he returned to Guernsey and so the possibility of him having to enlist might not arise at all. It was not that he was a coward, he reassured himself; simply that he did not approve of fighting when there should be a peaceful alternative.

With these thoughts dominating his mind, Ted managed very little sleep that night and also had difficulty concentrating on his duties in the joinery workshop during the following day.

Chapter 3

After rushing through tea with his family that evening, Ted grabbed his bicycle and instead of the usual left turn and cycling to meet Dick and Ruth at Cobo Bay, he turned right and cycled to the offices of the Guernsey Agriculture Council.

As he pedalled along, though, Ted began to have doubts that he would have much chance of being selected for the mission to America.

"I bet there'll be a queue of dozens wanting to get on that trip," he thought. "And most of them will be far better qualified for it than me."

However, as he rounded the last corner before the GAC offices, Ted was pleased to see a queue of only about half a dozen young men standing outside. He propped his bicycle against a nearby wall and took his place in the queue.

A further six or so young men soon joined behind Ted and as each one of them arrived, his optimism about his chances waned a little more.

"Not too many here, then," he observed to the chap ahead of him in the queue, albeit more to convince himself that there wasn't too much competition. "I'd have thought a few more lads would be keen to take up an opportunity to travel to America."

"Well, I reckon there must have been about two hundred at the Militia recruitment evening last week," the chap replied. "I suppose that shows that more of us want to go to fight the Hun than babysit a bunch of cows on a boat!"

Ted was surprised to hear this apparent reluctance for the adventure that might lie ahead and he questioned the lad as to why he was there in the queue if he really didn't want to do it.

"My family have farmed in Guernsey for generations and they really don't want our breed to fall into enemy hands," he said. "I work on the family farm and I owe it to my father to do this but rest assured, I'll be straight back here to sign-up to go to fight in France."

Ted realised that if the rest of the competition boasted similar experience, he was clearly going to need to be very 'creative' with his answers when he went inside for his interview.

After a few minutes, the door opened and the lads were invited to enter, one by one, and then they would each emerge about five minutes later and wait around in the street.

When it was Ted's turn, he was ushered in and invited to take a seat in front of three of the GAC committee members. The simple questions of name, age, height, weight, medical history and trade were easily negotiated and then his 'creativity' came into play.

"What experience do you have with cattle?" one of the panel asked him.

"My grandfather was a farmer and I spent many hours helping him with the cows," Ted replied, when the truth was that his grandfather Robins only farmed crops and the nearest that Ted had ever come to a cow was drinking milk and eating beef!

"Have you ever been seasick?" was the next question from the GAC panel.

"My other grandfather was a fisherman and I often went out in the boat with him," Ted replied, when really his only seafaring experience was messing about in a tiny rowing boat in Cobo Bay with Dick!

Ted was then told to wait outside with the others while a decision was made. After what seemed an eternity, but was actually only about half an hour later, the GAC chairman appeared in the doorway.

"I'll read out the names of the five who are going to America and they can come back inside to receive the itinerary for the journey," he announced. "To the rest of you, we thank you for your interest and we hope that you will now go to serve your island in France, instead."

The Chairman then proceeded to call out, in alphabetical order, the names of the five successful candidates — "Bichard, Bisson, Le Page, Robin and Tostevin."

Ted was immediately struck with two contrasting emotions: one of joyful surprise that he had been selected and the other of concern that his creative answers would soon be found out during the voyage.

Nevertheless, he collected his itinerary for the adventure ahead, which was scheduled to begin a week later, and he cycled home mentally preparing himself for the unenviable task of breaking the news to his father.

On entering the house, Ted saw that Nicholas, Elizabeth and Edith were enjoying a warm drink before retiring to bed and he decided to waste no time in telling them of his plans.

"You're doing what?" Nicholas boomed angrily. "We need our young men to fight in France and stop the Hun reaching our island, not to go swanning off on holiday!"

"Please keep your voice down," Elizabeth pleaded to her husband. "The other boys are asleep and they won't be fit for work if you wake them."

Ted managed to calm his father by pointing out that this was indeed an important mission in the service of their island. He also reassured Nicholas that it would detain him for only a few weeks and that he would then be returning to the island and joining the Guernsey Militia in France.

Although she would not say so to her husband, Elizabeth was quietly very relieved that her son might be spared the dangers of going off to war. However, she was also rather concerned that the journey to America could pose some dangers of its own.

Those feelings were quietly shared by Edith, who was saddened that she would not see her beloved Ted for some weeks, but she too was glad that he would be safe from the war and also fearful of what might confront him during this trip.

"It was only a couple of years ago that ship called the Titanic sank and so many people lost their lives," Elizabeth fretted. "You are not a strong swimmer, so how would you survive if the same thing happened to your boat?"

Ted reassured her that many ships had sailed to America since the Titanic and that none of them had suffered the same fate.

"And even if you do get to America safely," Edith chipped in, "the place is full of savages wanting to kill or torture you!"

"The problems with the red Indians are all well in the past," Ted told her. "They all live peacefully on reservations now and get on well with the white men who have settled in their country."

The respective reactions of Nicholas, Elizabeth and Edith were not shared by Billy and Charlie though, when their big brother told them of his news at the breakfast table the following day.

"Please be sure to keep a diary every day, Ted," Billy said. "Then I will be able to write it up into an article for the newspaper when you get back."

"You are so lucky to be getting the chance to sail on a big ship and seeing a new country," said an awe-struck Charlie. "I would so love to be going with you on such an adventure."

Greatly cheered by the encouraging comments from his brothers, Ted was able to work in the joinery that day in a much happier frame of mind, even though his father barely spoke a word to him throughout the day.

After tea that evening, Ted rushed to Cobo Bay and excitedly related to Dick and Ruth the details of his forthcoming adventure. He was pleased that Dick shared the Robins boys' enthusiasm for the whole idea, but he also understood that Ruth was sharing Elizabeth's concerns for his safety.

When the scheduled departure day arrived, Ted and the four other young men reported to the field where the cattle had been brought. The best cows and bulls from the island's cattle farms had been brought together to ensure that a top-quality herd was received in America.

Each of the lads had been told to bring a sack containing clothing, a spare pair of boots and one or two personal possessions (in Ted's case, he packed his Bible and a few of his woodworking tools). Their sacks were loaded onto a cart and the lads then shepherded the cattle behind the cart as it led them along the roads to the harbour and onto the boat that was to take them to Southampton.

Despite Ted's family and friends' varying emotions regarding his adventure, he was pleased to see that they had all come to the harbour to wish him well on his journey — even Nicholas!

"Take care and hurry back," Nicholas told his eldest son. "Even if the war is over by the time you return, I will still need you here to help me in the workshop."

Chapter 4

The voyage of about eighty miles from Guernsey to Southampton immediately exposed one of Ted's answers at his interview as being somewhat short of the truth.

Gale-force winds battered the small vessel as it ploughed through heavy seas and this provided clear evidence that Ted did indeed suffer from sea-sickness! However, there was little room to exercise the cattle and so Ted himself was spared the need to move around the boat very much.

Once they had safely docked in Southampton, the lads shepherded the cattle along the quay and then on to the much larger vessel that would take them across the Atlantic Ocean to New York.

Although the strong winds and rough seas were still prevailing as the ship made its way along the south coast of England, the size of the bigger vessel meant that the nauseous effect on Ted was rather less severe. And as the weather eased over the coming days, he felt more comfortable walking the cattle around the deck and giving them their feed and water.

However, another of Ted's creative answers at his interview was exposed when it came to milking the cows, as he had never done this and his early efforts were less than successful. But after some swift tuition from one of the other Guernsey lads, Ted soon mastered the technique and so that that particular untruth was soon laid to rest.

The paying passengers on the ship were treated to the best milk that they had ever tasted and it was clear that there would be a keen market for it when the cattle were settled in America.

Another problem of spending so much of the daylight hours on deck was Ted's pale skin. His rather sore sunburn in the early part of the voyage soon persuaded him to cover up and seek the shade as much as possible.

Other than the daily duties of exercising, feeding, watering, milking and mucking-out the cattle, the Guernsey lads had little else to do during the voyage. Ted was a fairly shy and quiet type and so, while the others chatted and played cards, he tended to spend most of his spare time reading his Bible.

Eventually the ship docked in New York. After due process had been completed at the Ellis Island Immigration Department, the Guernsey lads and their cattle were loaded into rail trucks for the journey to a ranch just outside the city of Philadelphia.

Crammed into wooden-sided rail trucks with the cattle was not only uncomfortable and smelly, but it also meant that the Guernsey lads were not able to see and appreciate the many miles of stunning scenery through which their train passed.

On arrival in Philadelphia, they shepherded the cattle many miles along roads and across open countryside until they eventually reached the ranch that would be the home of the Guernsey breed until the war in Europe was over.

Once the herd was settled, the young men from Guernsey were taken to a church hall in Philadelphia, where they would sleep for a couple of nights ahead of returning to New York and boarding a ship back to Southampton.

The lads used the time during those couple of days to explore Philadelphia and the surrounding area, walking many miles and being in awe of much of what they saw.

The roads were twice as wide as those in Guernsey and many of the buildings were very tall. There were also dozens of motor vehicles on the streets, whereas very few vehicles had ever been brought to their home island.

As Ted took a last walk on the day before the trip back to England, he came upon a large wooden building bearing a sign which read "Brook's Sawmill". He ventured closer and looked through the big gable doors, where he saw a dozen or so men using huge mechanical saws to strip and cut-to-length some of the biggest logs that Ted had ever seen in his life.

"Hey, what are you doing there?" the foreman shouted at Ted.

"Sorry, I'm a joiner by trade and I was just interested to see how you do things here," Ted reassured him.

"Ah, I can tell from your accent that you're not from these parts," said the foreman. "I guess you're one of those Englishmen I read about, in the newspaper, who've brought your cows here."

As a proud Guernsey man, Ted was not too keen to be described as an Englishman, but he opted not to make an issue of it and simply advised the foreman that he was quite correct.

"Well, if you're a joiner, we're always looking for experienced men," the foreman said. "If you are minded to stay in America and take a job here, come back and see me and we'll see what we can do."

Ted thanked the foreman and made his way back to the church hall. But as the other Guernsey lads chatted keenly about going home and the possibility of then going off to fight in France, Ted kept largely to himself and gave great thought to what the sawmill foreman had said.

Then, as the rest of them all rose and began to make their way to the door to begin their journey home, Ted asked them to stop and wait a moment as he had something important to say.

"I won't be coming back with you, lads," he said. "I've decided to stay in Philadelphia and try to make a new life for myself here."

"You can't do that," one of them retorted. "Everyone will think you're a coward if you don't come back."

"I am not a coward and I don't care what other people think," Ted replied. "This is my life and I will live it how I want."

After waving farewell to the other Guernsey lads at the train station, Ted made his way back to the sawmill and sought out the foreman.

"If that offer of a job is still there, I'd really like to take you up on it," Ted said.

"Sure, come into the office and we'll sort out the details," the foreman replied. "You can start work first thing tomorrow."

With the formalities completed, Ted commented to the foreman that he'd now need to find somewhere to live.

"Well, we've got a bunkhouse onsite, so you can bed down there if you've got nowhere else, but it does mean sharing with the other men," the foreman told him.

Ted was used to sharing sleeping quarters with his brothers at home and with the other Guernsey lads on the boat, so he was undeterred by the prospect. The foreman led him to a wooden shed alongside the main building, where a dozen narrow beds were lined up, six each side, with a small cupboard beside each one.

After a couple of weeks of shaping big logs into railway sleepers and telegraph poles, Ted became rather bored and began to wish that he could put his joinery skills into practice and make use of the tools that he had brought with him from Guernsey.

He had noticed that a daily bonfire dealt with the offcuts of wood from the sawmill and so he asked the foreman if he could take some of the unwanted wood in order to maintain his joinery skills in his spare time.

The foreman said that was no problem and Ted soon made himself a bigger and better cabinet to stand by his bed in the bunkhouse. When his 'room-mates' saw his new cabinet, they all asked him to make one each for them, too!

When Mr Brook, the sawmill owner, arrived on site one morning, he was intrigued to see a row of well-crafted cabinets leaning against the side of the bunkhouse. He asked the foreman about it.

"It's that new English guy making them from the offcuts of wood that would otherwise have ended up on the bonfire," the foreman advised his boss. "Don't worry, he's also doing it all in his spare time and not wasting any of the time that you pay him for."

"Well, I think perhaps he should be doing it in my time," said Mr Brook. "It's clear that this man has a talent that can be used to the benefit and profit of our company."

When Ted was summoned to the owner's office a short time later, he feared that his employment was about to be terminated. As he walked across there, he wracked his brains to try to think what he might have done wrong.

Imagine his delight, therefore, when Mr Brook explained that he was going to convert a currently redundant small shed on the site into a workshop for Ted and that he wanted him to make and sell his cabinets from there.

Chapter 5

The weeks went by and although feeling very happy with life, Ted realised that he had to confront one very difficult task: that of making contact with his family back in Guernsey. He had not wanted to burden any of the Guernsey lads with the unenviable task of telling Nicholas that his son was staying in America, so he decided to write a letter in which he told his family about his new life.

He took the letter to the mail office and sent it on its way across the Atlantic to his island home. However, the inter-continental postal service of 1915 wasn't what it is today and it took several weeks for his letter to reach Guernsey and then several more for a reply to arrive in Philadelphia. Sadly, the letter penned by his mother did not make happy reading.

"My dearest Ted,

While you may be very happy, you have caused great unhappiness here. Your father refuses to speak of you or allow any of the rest of the family to even mention your name.

He says that any further letters from you must go straight on the fire unopened.

I dearly want to stay in touch with you and so I will write to you without him knowing and I will let you know how things are here, but you must promise never to send another letter here.

Billy has signed up with the Militia and will soon be going off to France. He is just an ordinary soldier, not a war correspondent as he hoped, but I'm sure that won't stop him writing about it.

Charlie is desperate to join up and I fear that he too will go to fight in the war as soon as he has passed his sixteenth birthday.

Edith says she is missing you very much and hopes you may decide to return to Guernsey soon.

Your friends Dick and Ruth clearly are not missing you too much though as, only a week or so after I told Dick that you were staying in America, I heard that they are now a courting couple.

I'll write to you again when I can, but it may be only once a year, as your father will notice the money spent on the postage if I do it too often.

Take care, Son,

Your loving Mother."

Ted was upset, but not entirely surprised, to learn of his father's reaction and he was also concerned that his brothers were going to fight in the war in Europe. However, he found himself being more upset to learn that his trusted friends, Dick and Ruth, had wasted so little time in getting together in his absence.

As he gave more thought to it, though, Ted rationalised that as far as they knew he was never coming back to Guernsey and with the future occupation of the island still a possibility, it was perhaps quite reasonable for them to grow closer at that time.

Ted resolved to press on with adapting to his new life and to keep abreast of developments in Europe by way of the main newspaper in his area, the Philadelphia Herald. Along with most Americans though, he was shocked a short while later when a significant piece of news was reported.

The German Navy had sunk an American passenger ship, the Lusitania, with the loss of more than a thousand American lives and this outrage was causing widespread calls for America to enter the war.

Ted was desperate that the American politicians did not heed this call as, particularly being of British origin, he feared that it would be difficult for him to justify not signing up to go off to Europe with the US Army to help the Allied efforts against the German forces.

Over the ensuing months, Ted threw himself into his labours in his joinery workshop, though not simply making cabinets from superfluous wood. Mr Brook was now providing him with better-quality wood and this enabled Ted to branch out to create other items of furniture, such as beds, tables and chairs.

Mr Brook was delighted with Ted's work and began placing adverts in the Philadelphia Herald. Soon, many of the wealthier homeowners in the area were placing orders for Ted's furniture and this, in turn, began to create an impressive new income stream for the Brook business.

Being a fair and reasonable man, Mr Brook felt that Ted should be properly rewarded for his efforts and so, as well as increasing his weekly wage, he offered Ted a twenty-five per cent share in the income from the furniture sales.

With all of this going on in his life, Ted was able to dismiss any thoughts of enlisting in the American Army and instead, he strove to both build up the joinery business and to immerse himself in American life outside of his work.

Over the ensuing couple of years, Ted became a wealthy young man and was able to move out of the old wooden bunkhouse and buy himself an apartment in a fine, brick-built building on the outskirts of Philadelphia. He had maintained his Christian faith and became a regular attendee at a Methodist chapel in Philadelphia.

The furniture business expanded so much that Mr Brook invested in the construction of a larger workshop for Ted and he also appointed an apprentice to help him to manage the increasing workload.

Ted became a regular dinner guest at the Brooks' residence and he enjoyed playing with their three children; two boys of ten years and seven years, respectively, and a younger sister of four years. The games of football and cricket that he had enjoyed with his own brothers and Uncle Alf, back in Guernsey, were certainly not the staple diet of American children, but he still enjoyed the baseball games in the Brooks' garden.

Ted had also accepted Mr Brook's invitation to join his Gentlemen's Club, where he became an active member of the committee, charged with fund-raising for the less fortunate people living in Philadelphia and the surrounding area.

Everything in Ted's life seemed to be ticking along very nicely, but he was in for the biggest surprise of his life when a face from the past suddenly appeared.

Chapter 6

When the bell on his workshop door rang one day and Ted looked up, he couldn't believe his eyes when he saw Edith Breton standing before him!

"My God, Edith, is it really you?" Ted blurted out. "What are you doing here? How did you get here? What's going on?"

"Calm down, Ted," Edith laughed at his barrage of questions. "At least tell me that I'm looking well and that you're pleased to see me before you start demanding answers!"

Ted hugged his young aunt and cleared a seat for her, before pouring out a mug of water for each of them and then perching on the end of his work bench to listen, as she explained her arrival.

"I've missed you so much, Ted," she told him. "I've loved you and wanted to marry you for so many years and I just couldn't bear living in Guernsey without you. So I saved enough money for the fare, left a note for Elizabeth and here I am!"

Ted was stunned to learn that Edith had such deep feelings for him, particularly as he had never felt that way about her. He was even more amazed that she should be willing to undertake the arduous voyage to follow him to America, particularly as she was not physically robust and had never really enjoyed good health.

"Look Edith, I love you like a sister, but I've never thought of you as my future wife," he told her. "In fact, I don't think it's even legal for an aunt and nephew to get married!"

"You're probably right about that and if we were still in Guernsey, then it would not be possible," Edith conceded. "But this is America and nobody here knows that we are related, so we could get married here and I know that we can be very happy together here."

Before the conversation could continue, Mr Brook came into the workshop and was keen for Ted to reveal the identity of the pretty young woman.

"This is Edith Breton, an old schoolfriend of mine from Guernsey," Ted told him. "I wrote to tell her of my new life in America and she has decided to also try to make a better life for herself here."

"I'm delighted to meet you, my dear, and it may be that your arrival could be of great assistance to me and my wife," Mr Brook said. "We have a young family and we have recently resolved that my wife needs some help with them. Are you interested in taking up a position in our house as a live-in nanny to our children?"

Mr Brook had always been very impressed with Ted's honesty and work ethic, so he had no hesitation in assuming that any friend of Ted's would possess the same attributes.

"Thank you so much, sir," Edith enthused. "I certainly am very fond of children and I should very much like to accept your kind offer."

Edith's employment and accommodation issues had been resolved in one fell swoop and while she had harboured hopes of living with Ted immediately, she had realised that he would take some coaxing to warm to her desire for them to marry.

For his part, Ted was relieved that Mr Brook had provided an instant reprieve from the dilemma that Edith had sprung on him. He had not made any close friends since arriving in America and so he was delighted that he would now have Edith's company, but at the same time he was in a daze about her suggestion of marriage.

"Well, I had better take you along to meet my wife and get her approval," said Mr Brook. "But don't worry, I feel sure the two of you will get along just fine."

Mr Brook invited Ted over to his house for dinner that evening and then showed Edith out of the door and over to his motor car and they drove off to introduce her to his wife and children and to get her settled into their house.

It became apparent over the next few weeks that the arrangement was working very well for all concerned. Mr and Mrs Brook were delighted that Edith was very good with their children and the children were clearly soon very fond of her.

Ted and Edith were pleased that they were able to enjoy a good amount of time together, usually a couple of evenings a week and also at weekends. As the time went by, Edith began to feel that Ted was developing the kind of feelings for her that she had wanted for so long.

With sales of his furniture on the up, Ted treated himself to the purchase of an automobile and took Edith out for rides in the countryside, where they could have picnics and generally enjoy each other's company. They would often drive out to the ranch where the Guernsey cattle were living, which was a trip that always filled their heads with nostalgic memories of their island home.

As the months went by, Ted found himself falling in love with Edith and his concern that they were aunt and nephew seemed to pale into insignificance, particularly as they were the only people there who knew of that fact. They were able to enjoy a happy and fulfilling life in America, until another reminder of their roots arrived.

When Ted had written his letter to his family in Guernsey, a couple of years earlier, he had given the bunkhouse address on it. One day, the sawmill foreman came into Ted's workshop and handed him a letter that had been delivered there.

Although his mother had suggested she might write once a year, it was a full two years until Ted had received this next letter from her and this one made even more unhappy reading than the last.

"My dearest Ted,

I have had to summon up so much strength to write this letter to you and it grieves me to tell you this sad news.

Billy has been returned to us from France having suffered terrible injuries, the worst of which is that he has lost his sight. This is such a cruel blow for a boy who loved reading and writing so much.

He was hit by shrapnel and as well as his eyes, his chest was pierced and he now has such difficulty breathing, but at least he is still alive.

This terrible war is dragging on so much longer than anybody thought and nobody seems to be winning it.

The British line in the Somme hasn't moved in two years and all that happens is that our boys are being killed in their hundreds.

Charlie is over there now and I cry every day in fear that he may suffer a similar fate to Billy.

Edith left me a letter to say that she was going to travel to America to see if, like you, she could make a new life for herself over there.

Although your father would never agree, I am so glad that one of our sons and my little sister are both far away from the danger raging on this side of the Atlantic.

I hope that each of you will be able to find kind and loving people to settle down with and that you will both be able to live a full and happy life over there.

Take care Son,

Your loving Mother"

Ted was devastated to learn about Billy and was consumed with guilt that he had escaped from the horror that had enveloped his family. He showed the letter to Edith and she tried valiantly to console him, but Ted was equally guilt-ridden about his relationship with her. He started trying to see her less often, and instead, to spend his out-of-work hours on his church attendance, and his charity work.

Mr and Mrs Brook were concerned that Ted was visiting their house less often and asked Edith if there was a problem between them, but she reassured them that it was simply because of Ted's sorrow at the news about his brother.

As time went by and the guilt, on both counts, gradually eased, so Ted became again the relaxed and happy man that Edith knew and loved. They resumed their trips out in his car and soon their love began to blossom once again.

One day, as they stood among the Guernsey cattle, Edith got her dearest wish when Ted got down on one knee and asked her to marry him. Of course, she readily accepted his proposal and they set off to tell Mr and Mrs Brook of their plans.

"Edith has become like a member of our family during the last couple of years and we would very much like her to continue to help with our children, even if she will no longer be living in our house," Mr Brook told Ted. "Furthermore, we would also very much like to help with the arrangements for your wedding and also to contribute towards the costs."

Ted tried to protest that Mr Brook did not need to pay for the wedding and that he was able to take care of the cost himself, but his boss would hear none of it. Edith was just so elated that she would be able to live with Ted, and still work for Mr and Mrs Brooks, that she didn't mind who paid for the wedding as long as it happened!

The next few months saw Ted putting his Philadelphia apartment up for sale and the happy young couple then enjoyed viewing a number of houses as close as possible to the Brooks' residence.

Mr and Mrs Brook lived near a town called Radnor, which was in the county of Delaware, but still within the State of Pennsylvania. It was quite a considerable drive to and from Ted's workshop in

Philadelphia, but he was happy to make that lengthy daily commute in order to enable Edith to continue to work for them.

Once they had found a property they both really liked, and his flat was sold, so the plans began for their wedding. This was a chore that Ted and Mr Brook were more than happy to leave to the ladies.

Chapter 7

Business was booming, domestic life was good and Ted was beginning to think that life just couldn't get any better, when another letter from his mother arrived. He was immediately very concerned that this letter had come relatively soon after the previous one and his initial fears proved justified as he read its shattering content.

"My dearest Ted,

My heart is breaking as I write this letter to you. Charlie has been killed in action in France, alongside dozens of other young Guernsey men.

We cannot even pay our respects to his body, as he has been buried over there.

A decision has now been taken to withdraw the Guernsey Militia from France, as this island is in danger of losing a whole generation of menfolk.

Your father is devastated that one of his sons has died, while Billy is very depressed by his blindness and his crippled lungs.

I long to see both you and Edith again, but I know this will not happen and that I may never know whether you have found a wife and Edith has found a husband. I may never know whether I have any grandchildren or nieces and nephews.

However, that is a small price to pay in return for the knowledge that you are both safe and well and that you are free from the pain and tragedy that so curses our family.

Take care Son,

Your loving Mother"

Yet again a letter from Guernsey had shattered Ted's world and filled him with enormous guilt. He found himself seriously contemplating the option of he and Edith giving up their happy future in America and returning to Guernsey to care for his family. However, Edith was determined to convince him that this would be a terrible idea.

"If we went back there, we could never be married because everybody knows we're related and it would devastate Elizabeth to find out about our love for each other," she implored. "And why would we want to live on an island, which might be invaded by the enemy at any time, with a war raging only a few miles away?"

Edith pointed out to Ted that he was running a successful business in Philadelphia and that he would be letting Mr Brook down badly if he walked away from it now. Ted realised that his fiancée was right and that his first duty was to her and to the man who had done so much to help him to create a good life in America.

A few weeks later the wedding took place at the church in Radnor, with Mr Brook taking on the role traditionally fulfilled by the bride's father. His daughter was the only bridesmaid and Ted's apprentice was the best man. A lavish reception was held at the Brook's residence, from which Ted and Edith were quite relieved to escape as they dashed to catch a train for a brief honeymoon in New York.

There had been little time to see anything of New York when the Guernsey lads had unloaded the cattle there, three years or so earlier, and Ted was even more in awe of the scale of the buildings than he was of those when he first walked around the streets in Philadelphia.

On their return from honeymoon, the newly-weds moved into their new home and life ticked along quietly and happily. One day though, the Philadelphia Herald carried an article on the front page that Ted had been dreading.

Finally, almost two years after the sinking of the Lusitania, America had decided to enter the war in Europe and thousands of young men were to be sent across the Atlantic to support the British troops.

Ted again considered whether he should be playing his part, but the thought of what had happened to his two brothers, together with his fundamental conviction that war was evil, merely meant that Edith didn't need to work too hard this time to convince him to stay in America.

Within a year, the addition of the American troops had swung the advantage well towards the Allied forces in Europe and their victories on all fronts precipitated the abdication of Kaiser Wilhelm II. Mutinies within the German Navy soon followed and peace treaties were signed between Russia and Germany and between Austria and Italy.

Finally, on 11th November 1918, the Armistice was signed which brought the hostilities in Europe to an end. Then, in June 1919, the Treaty of Versailles was signed and committed all of the participating nations to live in peace henceforth.

Millions of lives had been lost during the four-year conflict, including thousands of young American men. So, while there were great celebrations and victory parades in cities and towns across the country, there was also an underlying anger among many that America had involved itself in a war so far away.

Back in Philadelphia, Ted Robin was a successful businessman with a nice home and lifestyle and a devoted wife. His apprentice was now fully trained and another apprentice had been taken on as the hand-built furniture business continued to thrive.

One thing that Ted and Edith had both hoped for was a family of their own, but after two years of marriage the couple had pretty much resigned themselves to remaining childless.

However, on 25th December 1919, when Mr and Mrs Brook had invited Mr and Mrs Robin to join them and their children for Christmas Day lunch, imagine everybody's surprise when Edith announced that she was pregnant!

"Doctor Griffiths says that because my own mother died giving birth to me, my confinement will need to be carefully managed," she told them. "But he is hopeful that, provided I cease work and rest and eat well, then we can expect a healthy child."

While Mr and Mrs Brook were disappointed to be losing their nanny, they were delighted for the young couple and readily offered their congratulations.

Ted was elated and spent the ensuing months following the doctor's orders to the letter, in fact almost being over-protective of his wife. Edith was often relieved when Ted went off to work, as it meant she could get up and walk around the house or sit in the garden without him fussing around her all the time.

Putting his joinery skills to personal use, Ted busied himself making a splendid crib for his new child, along with a wooden train set and an impressive scale-model of the ship that had brought him to America.

"I take it you are certain we will be having a son then," Edith laughed at him. "I'm really not sure a little girl will want to play with a boat and train!"

The summer of 1920 in Radnor was a very warm one, making the latter months of Edith's pregnancy rather uncomfortable. She found it difficult to sleep at night, while the humidity of the day caused nausea and breathing difficulties.

One night, seven months into the pregnancy, Edith woke Ted as she was showing signs of going into labour and he frantically ran the couple of streets to the doctor's house. Dr Griffiths swiftly attended the Robin's home and ministered to Edith in the bedroom upstairs while Ted then ran to alert Mr and Mrs Brook.

Mr Brook accompanied Ted back to his house and the pair of them tried to concentrate on a game of cards, while they waited nervously for Dr Griffiths to come downstairs. This vigil went on well into the night, until eventually the family doctor appeared, but the grim look on his face immediately told them that all was not well.

"What is the matter, Doctor? Please don't tell me that our baby hasn't survived. . ." Ted asked him, while barely wanting to hear the reply.

"Sadly, I regret to say that you are correct," Dr Griffiths confirmed. "But I am even more sorry to tell you that Edith's poor little body has also succumbed to the trauma of it all and she, too, has passed away."

Ted collapsed onto a chair as the awful news sank in. Another precious member of his family, perhaps the most precious of them all, had been taken from him. Mr Brook expressed his deepest sympathies to Ted and then set off back to his own house to break the awful news to his wife and their children.

Dr Griffiths told Ted that Edith had given birth to a stillborn baby girl and that he would make arrangements for their bodies to be collected the following day and taken to the chapel of rest.

The doctor took his leave and once Ted was left alone, he sobbed uncontrollably until desperate and irrational thoughts began to fill his mind. Was it him? Perhaps he was a jinx and anyone close to him was destined to an early death? Perhaps God was punishing him for marrying his aunt? Perhaps God was punishing him for deserting his family and his island home?

Sorrow and depression overwhelmed Ted throughout the following day, particularly as he watched the bodies of his wife and baby being placed into the same coffin and taken away on the back of a cart.

The church minister called round later in the day to discuss the funeral arrangements with Ted, but his mind was really not concentrating on the matter in hand and he just agreed to whatever the minister proposed.

One thing Ted was able to decide without thought, though, was when the minister asked for the name of the child. He immediately said that his daughter was called Elizabeth after his mother. Ted had always been convinced that they would have a son and therefore girls' names had not really been discussed, but Ted felt sure that Edith would very much approve of his choice.

Another day went by and then Ted had to go through the ordeal of the funeral. The coffin was loaded onto a horse-drawn hearse and a small procession of mourners followed it on foot as it made its way from the chapel of rest to the church, where Edith and Ted had been married only three years earlier.

Ted managed to hold himself together as he delivered a Bible reading during the funeral service. He also remained stoic as he watched the coffin containing his beloved Edith and their tiny daughter being lowered into a grave in the cemetery alongside the church.

Although it was normal practice for the mourners to gather for light refreshment after a funeral, Ted just couldn't bring himself to attend that and left Mr and Mrs Brook to host the event. He climbed into his motor car and drove out to the ranch where the Guernsey cattle were still in residence.

Although the deal had been for the cattle to be returned to their island of origin after the war in Europe was over, the authorities in Guernsey had no longer seen this as a priority. The island had not been invaded and its unique herd had not been diluted or culled and it was therefore considered far more important to strive to rebuild the local community, particularly given that the heavy losses in Northern France had deprived the island of so many of its young men.

As he gazed at the cattle, Ted's mind was again filled with happy memories of his early years in Guernsey. He recalled the lovely evenings on the beach at Cobo with his friends and playing football with his uncle and brothers in the field behind their home. All of this again invoked a strong sense of duty in Ted that he ought to return, across the Atlantic to Guernsey, to take care of his family there.

Chapter 8

Thoughts of his family in Guernsey continued to occupy Ted's mind over the ensuing days until, after much soul-searching, he went to Mr Brook's office and told him that he had decided that he wanted to leave America and return to Guernsey.

"I'm so sorry, but I feel that there is nothing here for me now, whereas I have family who need me to be there for them," he said.

"There is your wife and daughter's grave here and there is your duty to continue our business relationship," Mr Brook retorted sharply.

"I'm sorry, but visiting their grave is just too painful an experience to put myself through, week in and week out, for the rest of my life," Ted told him. "As for the business, there are two good joiners there now to carry on the work, so you don't really need me any more."

The men continued to debate the issue for some time, but eventually Mr Brook had to accept that Ted's mind was made up and he was not going to be dissuaded from the path that he intended to take.

Ted put his house up for sale and it took only a matter of a few weeks for a good offer to arrive for it and he readied himself to leave America. One sad chore he undertook before leaving his home for the last time was to build a bonfire in the garden, on which he destroyed the crib, train set and model ship that he had made for his child.

In addition to the profit made from the proceeds of the house-sale, once he had cleared the balance of the mortgage, Ted also received twenty-five per cent of the profit on sales from the furniture store during the past year. He was therefore able to wire ahead a tidy sum to a bank in Guernsey with which to assist his parents and brother when he returned to the island.

Mr Brook drove Ted to the railway station in Pennsylvania and his wife and children went along too. Ted embraced them all and then shook hands with Mr Brook and thanked him for all that he had done for him since he arrived there six years earlier.

As Ted boarded a passenger carriage on the train to New York, he smiled to himself that this was rather more comfortable than sharing a rail-truck with cattle as he had done when he first travelled between the two places.

The voyage across the Atlantic between New York and Southampton was also a good deal more pleasant this time, as Ted was able to book a nice clean cabin rather than being cramped up in a tiny cot and surrounded by cows.

On arrival in Southampton, Ted reasoned that he would be unlikely to leave Guernsey again for quite some time once he had settled back there and so he allowed himself a few days in which to explore Southampton, Winchester, the Isle of Wight and other sights in the area. He then took a train from Southampton to Weymouth and from there boarded a ferry for the final leg of his journey home.

Standing on the deck as the Channel Islands loomed into view in the early morning light, Ted was filled with much happiness and as soon as he disembarked from the boat, once it had berthed alongside the quay at St Peter Port harbour, he immediately felt at home.

As he strolled along, he noticed that most of the buildings had remained much as they were when he last saw them. He also noticed that the island had acquired a handful of taxi cabs, but as it was such a fine day, he elected to walk the couple of miles up the hill from the port and along the road to his family home.

On the way he noted that there were now several other motor vehicles on Guernsey's roads, primarily commercial vans and lorries, but also a few private cars. It was just as he reached the top of the long hill up from the harbour that a lorry slowed down alongside him and a familiar voice called out.

"Blimey, if it isn't the old ghost come back to haunt us," teased the bronzed individual behind the wheel. "I better give you a lift before you burn up in the sun!"

"Hello Dick. You haven't lost that useless sense of humour, then," Ted laughed back at his old friend. "Mind, I see you've graduated from driving a horse and cart!"

Ted threw his suitcase into the back of Dick's lorry and clambered into the cab and the two men shook hands warmly, immediately knowing that time had not dimmed their affection for each other and that their friendship remained intact.

As they drove along, Dick told Ted that he had married Ruth and that they had a two-year-old son and another child on the way. He also told Ted that he had taken over the running of his father's business and that life was going very well for him and his family.

"I'll tell you what, do you remember that house called Rockmount at Cobo Bay?" Dick asked. "Well, it's now a hotel and bar and I usually pop in there for a beer on the way home from work every evening. Why don't you come down there tonight for a couple of pints and you can tell me all about your glamorous life in America?"

Coming from a religious background and given his father's disapproval of Uncle Alf's liking for public houses and beer, Ted had never tried alcohol when he was living in Guernsey and he had maintained that abstinence throughout his time in America.

Hence, the thought of drinking beer with Dick presented him with some concern, so Ted used the excuse that he really ought to spend his first evening back in Guernsey with his family. To ensure that his old friend wasn't offended though, Ted said that he would join Dick for a drink one evening later in the week.

Dick dropped Ted outside the Robin family home and as he retrieved his luggage from the back of the lorry and said goodbye to his friend, Ted immediately noticed that the sign above the workshop door had reverted from the *"N Robin & Son — Master Joiners"* to *"N Robin — Master Joiner"*.

As he entered the house, Elizabeth burst into tears of joy and dashed to embrace her eldest son. She complimented Ted on how well he looked and then looked beyond him and asked, "Where's Edith?"

Ted then broke the news to his mother that her little sister had died and that this had prompted his decision to return to Guernsey to be with his family. He did not tell her of the marriage or that Edith had died in childbirth, instead telling Elizabeth that her sister had succumbed to TB.

Elizabeth was deeply upset, but composed herself, and then led Ted into the kitchen where William was sitting at the table and polishing a pair of boots as best his blind eyes would let him. Ted went across and tenderly placed a hand on his brother's shoulder.

"Hello Billy, it's Ted," he said. "I've come back to be with my family and it is so good to see you again."

William was overjoyed to hear his brother's voice and jumped up to hug him, but the sudden excitement triggered one of his convulsive coughing fits and Ted was very alarmed to see how badly Billy struggled for breath. Elizabeth came forward and eased Billy back down into his chair and proceeded to gently pat and rub his back until the coughing subsided.

"He's fine when he is calm and relaxed," Elizabeth assured Ted. "It's just too much excitement, like you've just given him, that makes these horrible attacks occur."

"Okay, I'll make myself scarce for a while then," said Ted. "I take it Father is in the workshop?"

"Yes, but he is certainly not going to welcome you back with open arms," Elizabeth warned. "You hurt him deeply by deciding to stay in America and I really don't think he'll be in the mood for forgiveness just yet."

Hence, Ted was prepared for a less than warm response from Nicholas, but he was still very shocked by the severity of his father's hostility. When the bell above the workshop door tinkled and Nicholas turned to see who was there, the immense rage that had festered within him over the years took very little time to rush to the surface.

"How dare you show your face here! You are not welcome in my workshop and you are not welcome in my house!" he bellowed at Ted. "Now get out of here before I really lose my temper and throw you out!"

"I know you will never forgive me for what I've done in the past, but please allow me to now help with the present and the future," Ted appealed to his father. "I have returned with plenty of money to help you to support Mother and William and I can also help you here in the workshop again."

"I don't want your money and you will never work in here again!" Nicholas roared, but the mention of his wife did at least cause him to consider her feelings and to grudgingly offer a form of compromise. "For the sake of your mother and brother, I will allow you to visit my house occasionally to see them, but as far as I am concerned you mean nothing to me and you never will."

As he left the workshop, Ted struggled to contain his great sadness at his father's hostility towards him and so decided to call on his Uncle Alf two doors away rather than let his mother see him so upset.

As he walked the few yards to Alf's bicycle shop, Ted vaguely noticed a 'For Sale' sign in the window of his grandparents' cottage, but his mind was too occupied with his father's words to think much of it.

In stark contrast to the reaction from Nicholas, Alf was absolutely delighted to see his eldest nephew again and welcomed him with a huge smile and hearty handshake.

"Well, look what the cat's dragged in," he teased. "The prodigal son returns, but I bet my brother hasn't welcomed you back in the same way as that father in the Bible!"

Ted advised his uncle that his father had effectively disowned him and had banned him from returning to live in the family home. "Oh yes, speaking of which, why is there a 'For Sale' sign next door on Granny and Grandpa's cottage?" Ted asked his uncle.

"Alas, as if we didn't lose enough of our population to the war, I'm sorry to tell you that both your grandparents have passed away during the last year or so," Alf replied. "I am not desperate for the money, but your father's business is not doing too well and so we need to sell the cottage. Unfortunately, there are very few people around who can afford it and so it has stood empty since they died."

Although naturally saddened to hear that both of his grandparents had passed away, Ted was very interested to hear that their home was empty and available. He asked his uncle for the price of the cottage and was very pleased to learn that it was just a little less than the amount of money he had wired back from America.

"That has sorted out my accommodation problem and also my father's financial problems then," Ted said. "I will buy the cottage and then I will be able to provide funds for my family in that way without my father raging that I am insulting him by offering him charity."

While they agreed that Nicholas would be far from happy to sell his parents' cottage to his estranged son, they also reasoned that he could hardly refuse to do so as his own financial situation was very far from rosy.

"The other priority for me now is to go out and look for a job and to do that I'm going to need some transport," Ted told Alf. "Would you mind if I take a bicycle from you today and I will pay for it once I've been to the bank to sort out the money to buy the cottage?"

Alfred was not only happy with that arrangement, but he also gave Ted the key to the cottage and told him to make himself at home in there straight away. The cottage had been closed up for a long time and virtually all of the furniture had been sold.

For the rest of the day therefore, Ted busied himself with airing the place, sweeping and dusting and all the while recalling the happy times he had spent in that cottage when he was a child.

Chapter 9

As the evening approached and still rather rattled by his father's words, Ted decided that he would join Dick for a drink after all. He grabbed his newly-acquired bicycle and rode down to Cobo Bay to see if Dick was indeed at the Rockmount Hotel.

Sure enough, parked outside the hotel was a lorry with 'W Birdsall & Son' written along the side of it and Dick was pleased to see his old friend again so soon.

Dick bought them a pint of beer each and Ted barely noticed the taste or intoxicating effect of it as he told Dick about his father's reaction to his home-coming, about how he planned to buy his grandparents' cottage and about his need to find a job.

"Ah, well, I think I can probably help you on that last point. Can I assume that you learnt to drive a motor vehicle when you were in America?" Dick asked. Ted confirmed that he had indeed done so and that he had owned his own car.

"In that case, that's your job problem sorted out, too," said Dick. "You can come to work for me, collecting the crops from the vineries and delivering them down to the harbour."

"I'm sorry, but you can't just give me a job because we're old friends," said Ted. "That wouldn't be fair on all the other men on the island who need employment."

"Listen Ted, the war wiped out a good number of our young men and of those remaining, very few of them are able to drive a lorry," Dick told him. "So, to tell the truth you are a God-send for my business and I would be very grateful if you can start first thing tomorrow morning."

Duly satisfied that he was being offered employment on his merits rather than purely out of friendship, Ted was then happy to accept Dick's offer and the two men duly celebrated with another pint of beer and continued to chat for another hour or so.

Dick knew that Edith had left Guernsey to follow Ted to America and duly asked if they had indeed met up over there. Ted confirmed that Edith had tracked him down and that she had also settled in the Philadelphia area. However, he told Dick that Edith had died of TB shortly before his return to Guernsey and again, he did not reveal that they had been married.

Ted woke up the following morning with a thumping headache and quickly realised that he had only half-an-hour to get to the depot of W Birdsall & Son on time to start his first day at work there.

The depot was located in St Sampson's, which was the island's second town and the site of the harbour for cargo vessels, as opposed to the passenger boats that sailed into St Peter Port.

Faced with a four-mile cycle ride to get to the depot, Ted threw on some clothes and splashed some water on his face before dashing out of the cottage and racing off on his new bicycle.

"Oh, that's a good start, late on your first day," Dick mocked as Ted skidded into the yard about five minutes after his due start time. "I can see that I'm going to need to keep a sharp eye on your time-keeping, young man!"

"It's entirely your fault because you forced me to drink strong ale last night," Ted snapped back at his friend. "I haven't even had time for any breakfast, thanks to you, although I'm not sure it would stay down if I did!"

Dick laughed and led Ted into his office in the corner of the yard and gave him a sheet of paper containing the addresses of four vineries, before taking him outside again and pointing to one of the lorries in the yard.

"Take that one and you should be able to get two of the jobs done this morning and the other two this afternoon, so you should have time for a nice greasy lunch," he teased. "Just make sure you get back here before dusk though, because that lorry doesn't have headlights like your fancy American car!"

Ted soon found that he really enjoyed driving around the quiet roads and lanes of Guernsey compared to driving on the busier thoroughfares of Philadelphia. That said, having worked in a joinery workshop all of his adult life, he did find the loading and unloading of the fruit and flower boxes very tiring and this did make his arms ache by the end of the day.

At the end of his first working day for W Birdsall & Son, Ted accepted a lift from Dick, whose own lorry did have headlights, along to the Rockmount Hotel. On this occasion though, he confined himself to just a glass of lemonade, before retrieving his bicycle from the back of Dick's lorry and setting off on the uphill ride home to the well-earned comfort of his bed.

In the coming days, Alf and Ted arranged an appointment to see a lawyer in St Peter Port and the deeds for the purchase of the cottage were duly prepared. Ted made the necessary arrangements with his bank for the transfer of funds and, although Nicholas was indeed less than happy when the identity of the purchaser was revealed, he nevertheless accepted the welcome injection of funds into his coffers.

As the winter nights rolled in, the after-work socialising with Dick fizzled out, due to the less pleasant cycle rides home on the cold, dark nights. However, Ted was then able to spend his evenings making all of the furniture for his new home.

Considering it a waste of his joinery skills not to do so, Ted had even thought of starting up his own joinery business, but he realised that setting up in competition with Nicholas would be damaging to his father's business. He was also quite happy with the outdoor life that came with working for Dick, so he resolved to confine himself to just undertaking carpentry as and when it was required for his own property.

One routine that Ted did find himself falling into though, was agreeing to join Alfred at The Beehive each Saturday night. Although Ted confined himself to just one pint of beer during these evenings, Alfred would proceed to enjoy several large whiskies and Ted regularly had to support his uncle as they walked home.

After a while, Ted asked Dick if he could use his lorry for a few hours each Sunday to take Billy out for drives. Dick was quite happy to agree to this arrangement and even refused Ted's offer to pay for any fuel that he used while doing so.

These outings provided a source of great joy for Billy, who was now once again able to smell the sea air, feel the sandy beaches between his toes and generally enjoy being able to use those senses that remained available to him. However, Ted did have to ensure that the speed at which he drove the lorry did not cause too much of a breeze to blow into Billy's face, as this could trigger severe coughing fits and considerable discomfort for his brother.

Chapter 10

Ted's life continued in similar vein for a year or so, until one day he had to cover another driver's round. This involved calling at a small vinery in the parish of Torteval in the south-west corner of the island. Ted had not been to this vinery before and as he was loading boxes of tomatoes onto his lorry, he noticed two teenage girls sitting on a wall nearby and watching him while he worked.

"Hey there — if you've nothing better to do than sit on the wall, you can come over here and help me to load this lot," he teased them.

While the girls declined Ted's invitation to share some of the work, they did wander over and engage in conversation with him. It transpired that they were seventeen-year-old Frances Gallen and her fifteen-year-old sister, Marie, and they were the daughters of the tomato grower whose boxes Ted was collecting.

As they chatted happily, Frances told Ted that she was shortly to start her first paid job as a maid in a large property called Catel House.

"I know Catel House. It's only about a mile from my home," Ted said. "But it must be at least five miles from here, so that's a long way for you to go there and back every day, isn't it?"

"Yes, it's going to be a long walk each morning and evening to start with, but I hope to earn enough money in the first few months to be able to buy myself a bicycle," Frances told him.

Marie decided that she was now bored and wandered off to do something else, but Frances and Ted continued to chat away until he suddenly realised that he would be late delivering her father's produce to the harbour if he didn't get a move on.

He wished Frances a good evening and set off apace in his lorry, but he could not stop thinking about her as he drove along. Even though he was now twenty-eight years of age — more than ten years older than Frances — he found himself quite captivated by her.

On the following Monday morning, when he arrived for work, Ted saw the driver who usually did the pick-up from the Gallen vinery and suggested to him that he was happy to do that job on Saturdays in addition to his own round. His colleague was pleasantly surprised by Ted's offer and only too happy to take him up on it as it enabled him to get home much earlier than usual.

However, not content with just being able to see Frances at her home in Torteval on Saturdays, Ted also changed his route home on weekday evenings in order to take him past Catel House. It soon became normal routine for Ted to meet Frances as she came out of work and to give her a lift home on the crossbar of his bicycle. Of course, this only served to double his own journey, but he was happy to arrive home later and even more tired if it meant he could enjoy the company of his new friend.

This arrangement brought an end to Ted and Dick's ritual of enjoying a pint in the Rockmount after work each evening and also curtailed Ted accompanying Alfred to The Beehive on a Saturday night.

However, although Ted and Frances were enjoying themselves and Dick and Alf were resigned to not having Ted's company as much, as a result, not everybody was entirely comfortable with the budding relationship.

Bert Gallen, Frances' father, was initially less than pleased about it as he considered Ted to be far too old and worldly wise for his innocent young daughter. So, one day when Ted was collecting tomato boxes from his vinery, Bert decided to tackle him about it.

"Listen, Ted. Frances has spent all her life out here in Torteval and has rarely even been in to St Peter Port. Apart from playing the organ in our parish church and attending the parish school, she had rarely set foot off my property until she got that job at Catel House," he said. "She tells me that you are more than ten years older than her and that you have travelled to America, so I'm really not sure that she's ready for a relationship with somebody like you."

Ted tried to reassure Mr Gallen that his intentions towards Frances were entirely honourable and he even volunteered to have Marie come along as a chaperone on their 'dates'. Of course, Marie couldn't be there when Ted was giving Frances a lift home from work on his bicycle, but the fact that he had at least offered to have her sister come along at all other times did seem to placate her father.

On learning that Frances played the organ at the Torteval parish church, and given that he had to endure his father's glare and silence every Sunday at his own family's church in St Peter Port, Ted decided to ask Mr Gallen if he would mind if he switched to attending the Torteval church with his family, instead.

This was another shrewd move in the strategy of winning Mr Gallen's approval and trust, particularly when Ted also showed a willingness to sometimes read a lesson during the services.

However, the perk of taking a lorry home from work on Saturday evenings soon became used for a different purpose from that originally intended. Instead of taking his brother Billy out for rides in the lorry, Ted began to use it to drive to Torteval Church and then, after the service, to drive Frances and Marie around the island and show them some places that they had never or rarely seen before.

After some weeks, Frances had saved up enough money to buy a bicycle and Ted offered to take her to choose one at his Uncle Alf's shop. Thereafter, the two of them would ride side-by side each evening from her place of work to her home, chatting away as they went and getting to know each other better.

Although Ted told Frances about his trip to America and about various things that happened during his time there, he did not tell her anything about Edith or their stillborn child. After all, he had not even told his mother or anybody else in Guernsey about that part of his life and had resolved that he would keep it to himself forever.

It was in the early spring of 1922, that Ted decided to ask Mr Gallen for his daughter's hand in marriage. He managed take him aside and speak to him, away from anyone else's hearing range, as they left the church one Sunday morning.

Mr Gallen repeated his concern that Ted was much older than Frances, but he then said that he could see that Ted cared deeply for her and that the manner in which Ted had conducted their courtship was much appreciated by him and his wife. He said that he would therefore give his blessing and they returned to join the rest of the family.

"Ted and Frances will be taking a drive without you today," Mr Gallen told Marie. "I think they need a little time to themselves on this occasion."

Frances was quite surprised by what her father had said and began to fear that he was allowing them to go off together so that Ted could explain to her in private that he could not see her any more

They climbed into the cab of his lorry and as they drove off, Frances asked Ted what he had been discussing with her father outside the church. Ted told her that he would explain once they reached Cobo Bay. Having parked and made their way down the steps onto the beach, they began strolling along the beach and then Ted suddenly dropped to one knee.

"This is my favourite place in the world and so this is where I wanted to ask my favourite person in the world to be my wife," he blurted out. "Your father has given me permission to ask you to marry me and so I hope you will do me that honour."

Frances was absolutely delighted, both at Ted's proposal and also that her father had eased his fears about their age-gap. She readily accepted Ted's proposal and they ran up the beach and into the lorry and drove back to the Gallen house to tell the rest of the family their news.

"I'm afraid we are not wealthy people and so this wedding won't be a very grand affair," Bert Gallen told Ted.

"That's fine by me," Ted assured him, remembering the rather lavish wedding in Radnor that Edith and Mrs Brook had organised and feeling very relieved that he would not have to endure all that palaver again.

However, Mr Gallen did insist on the wedding not taking place until after his daughter had reached her eighteenth birthday. So, while Ted and Frances were both very keen to begin their married life together, they had to respect her father's wishes and to set a date for around a year ahead.

When Ted went home that evening and popped next door to tell his mother about the wedding, she said that she would be happy to utilise her needlework skills to make the bridal gown for Frances and also a bridesmaid's dress for Marie. Ted reported this to Frances the next time he saw his fiancée and she was delighted to accept, as was her father as it meant a bit less expense for him!

A few days later, Ted introduced Frances to his mother and brother and Uncle Alf, and they met again several times during the ensuing months at dress-fitting sessions, when Ted was delighted to note how well they all got on together. Frances did think it was unfortunate that she could not meet Ted's father, but he had explained the circumstances to her and she just had to accept that this was just how things were.

Chapter 11

Eventually the wedding day arrived and as everyone gathered at the Torteval parish church, Ted was rather embarrassed by the lack of guests on his side of the church. Nicholas had refused to attend and so Alfred had brought Elizabeth and William to the ceremony in his van. Dick fulfilled the role of best man, while Ruth and their two small children were the only other guests in the pews on the Robin side of the aisle.

By contrast, Mr and Mrs Gallen had not only two daughters, but also three sons and a host of brothers and sisters, aunts and uncles and cousins. There was also a good turnout from their many friends among the community of the parish of Torteval.

A honeymoon was certainly not something that a young couple in Guernsey could afford in 1925, so Ted and Frances moved straight into his little cottage on their wedding night. Frances then spent the ensuing few weeks, with Elizabeth's help and guidance, making curtains and cushions and generally turning what had been Ted's rather drab 'bachelor pad' into a comfortable and cosy home for a newly-wed couple.

Ted had insisted that she give up her job as a maid at Catel House, light-heartedly assuring her that he would always provide for her while she fulfilled the far more important duty of being his maid and not somebody else's!

During those first few weeks of marriage to Frances, Ted grew more and more convinced that he had never been happier and that the immense highs and lows of emotion that he had experienced over the past decade or so, both in Guernsey and in America, were now well behind him.

He had lost his wife and child, he had lost his youngest brother, his other brother had been severely wounded and his father had disowned him. However, the very painful memories of all of those sad events were now considerably eased by the immense joy of being with Frances.

Ted was also very pleased to see that his new bride got on so well with Dick and Ruth. The two couples would meet up at the beach and Frances would play happily with the Birdsall's two children, building sand-castles, exploring rock-pools and helping them to learn to swim. The foursome would also enjoy meals together at each other's houses and the occasional trip to watch black and white silent movies at the island's newly opened cinema in St Sampson's.

Once more though, Ted's bliss was to be shattered and he would again find himself questioning whether he and the people he loved were being punished because of his behaviour.

As he and Frances were saying goodbye to each other on the doorstep of their cottage, as he was setting off for work one morning, Ted noticed Doctor Lawrence emerging from his parents' house next door and rushed to ask him who was ill.

"I'm sorry Mr Robin, but I regret to inform you that your brother must have had one of his convulsions during the night and it seems that he choked on his own vomit," the doctor solemnly advised. "I'm afraid he has passed away and your poor parents are obviously greatly distressed at this time."

Ted dashed into the house and straight to his mother, who was sobbing at the kitchen table, while his father stared silently out of the widow. While embracing his mother, Ted suggested to his parents that they could leave all of the funeral costs to him.

"No thank you very much. I am quite capable of arranging and paying for my own son's funeral without any help from an outsider!" Nicholas replied abruptly.

"For God's sake, Nicholas, can you not at least be civil to your eldest son when we are all mourning the loss of another?" Elizabeth wailed.

"Surely there is no better time to forgive and forget the past and for what's left of our family to come together to support each other?"

If it had not been for his wife's distress, Nicholas would have remained resolute in his rejection of Ted, while Ted had grown so ambivalent to the disapproval of his father that if it had been left to the two men, they would have agreed to never speak again.

However, both of them were filled with compassion for Elizabeth and there was a silent nod between them to agree that they would temporarily put their differences aside for her sake.

Ted left his parents to their grief and sadly climbed aboard his bicycle to continue his journey to the depot at W Birdsall & Son, where he told Dick what had happened.

"Look, there's no need for you to work today, Ted," Dick told his friend. "Go home and look after your parents and your wife and I'll cover your round today."

But Ted knew that his father did not want him there at all, so he declined Dick's kind offer and instead insisted that he carried on with his normal duties.

When he arrived home that evening, Ted confided to Frances that he felt so very guilty for giving up on taking Billy out for Sunday drives in the lorry.

"I really should have continued to spend more time with him and to have shown him that he was still very important to me," Ted lamented. "So often I have been selfish and put myself first, when I should have shown more consideration for my family."

A few days later, a small gathering attended Billy's funeral at St Stephen's Church and the second of Nicholas and Elizabeth's three sons was laid to rest. There was no 'wake' (unlike Edith's funeral in America), largely because there was only Nicholas and Elizabeth, Ted and Frances and Uncle Alf at the funeral.

As the weeks went by, Frances was concerned that her husband's guilt about neglecting his brother during their courtship was making the early months of their married life rather less enjoyable than they should have been. Ted was coming straight home from work and after eating dinner in relative silence, he would sit and read his Bible until it was time for bed. He was no longer interested in trips to the beach or cinema with Dick and Ruth, and apart from going to work and attending church on Sundays, he barely even ventured out of the house.

Her understanding and patience paid off though, as gradually Ted began to pull himself together and become his old self again. He resolved to himself that he would pay more attention to

Frances and he made a determined effort to help her as much as possible around the house. They became closer again as he increasingly ensured that he put her first in everything he did.

Indeed, apart from popping next door a couple of times a week to spend some time with his mother, when Nicholas wasn't around, Ted became a very devoted and loving husband and Frances began to realise the aspirations she had when she agreed to become his wife.

Chapter 12

Five years seemed to race by as Ted and Frances enjoyed their life together. Ted did resume joining Dick for a pint at The Rockmount after work, but only on Friday nights, and he also resumed meeting Alfred for a pint in The Beehive on Saturday nights.

Frances was happy for her husband to enjoy a social life outside of the home on a couple of evenings a week, as she recalled how depressed he had been in the months following Billy's death and how he had shunned virtually all contact with friends and family.

The couple also remained very close to the Gallen family and, most weeks, enjoyed Sunday lunches with them after the morning service at Torteval parish church.

One day in the summer of 1930, as if his life could become any more content, Ted came home from work to receive some very unexpected news from Frances.

"I've been to see Doctor Lawrence today and it seems we are to become parents," she told Ted.

"Some time towards Easter we will be blessed with an addition to our family."

After five years of marriage and no pregnancy, Ted and Frances had resigned themselves to the fact that they were not to be blessed with children and, although he was initially delighted by the happy news from Frances, it also then caused a mixture of emotions to well up inside him as he began to recall the tragic events resulting from his first wife's pregnancy.

As the weeks and months went by, Ted seemed to grow less and less interested in the impending arrival and eventually Frances lost her patience and confronted him.

"What on earth is the matter with you?" she shouted at him. "We are about to have our first child and you don't seem to want to know anything about it!"

Frances was then completely taken aback when Ted collapsed in tears and blurted out that he was absolutely terrified of losing both her and their baby.

"Why on earth would you possibly have such fears?" Frances asked. "I am young and fit and healthy and Doctor Lawrence says that all is well with my pregnancy."

After all the years of keeping his American secret to himself, Ted finally resolved that he owed it to Frances to tell her the truth. So he sat his young wife down and asked her to promise that she would never repeat to another living soul what he was about to tell her.

Once she agreed, Ted then related how he and Edith had grown close after she followed him to America, how they had married and how she had died giving birth to their stillborn daughter.

"Every time I get a bit of really good news in my life, it has been swiftly followed by some tragic event befalling somebody I love," Ted lamented. "You are the most precious thing in my life and I can't bear the thought that the jinx of Ted Robin will cause you any harm."

Frances was stunned to learn that the man she loved had been married before, particularly to his own aunt, and that he had kept this a secret from her and from his parents. But she soon came to terms with this unexpected development and firmly reassured Ted that it made no difference to her or to the future wellbeing of their little family.

"Now listen here. You, me and this baby are all going to have a long and wonderful life together," she told him. "The Ted Robin jinx, if it ever existed, is now well in the past and we are never going to speak of it again."

Although Ted agreed to erase his dreadful past experiences from the equation, he also resolved to himself that he would not make the same preparations as he had done when Edith was expecting. Back in Radnor, he had decorated the baby's room, made a crib and made some toys, but he did none of those things on this occasion.

In the early hours of 27th January 1931, Ted believed his greatest fear was about to happen when Frances woke him to say that she thought the baby was coming. Just like Edith, Frances was going into labour about two months early and Ted dreaded that this meant that the same tragedy was about to unfold.

He dashed next door and summoned his mother to assist Frances in her labour and then he sat on the garden wall in the cold night air to wait for news. As daylight dawned, Elizabeth came to the door and told Ted to run to fetch the doctor, who lived only five minutes away, as she was concerned that the birth was not going to be straightforward.

Ted could not contain his fears and burst into tears as he ran along the road. He hammered on Doctor Lawrence's front door and could barely speak when the doctor opened it, but he managed to blurt out what he needed to say and soon the two of them were running back towards Ted's cottage.

Doctor Lawrence went inside and Ted sat and waited on the garden wall again. After a while, Alfred looked out of his window and spotted his nephew. He went outside and ascertained the situation from Ted and then told him that there was only one course of action in these circumstances.

"You and me are going to play football in the field," he informed Ted and so the two of them trooped off through the bicycle shop and out onto the field that ran behind the Robin properties, collecting a ball on their way.

They proceeded to run, tackle and shoot as they had done twenty years before and this continued for quite some time, until Elizabeth called from the back door of the cottage for them to come indoors. Ted again felt the tears welling up as he feared the worst and tried to prepare himself for terrible news.

"Congratulations, Ted, you have a fine son," the doctor informed him. "He was born very early and so he is a bit small and weak, but I'm sure that he is healthy and will soon grow into a strapping lad."

Naturally delighted to hear that his child had survived the birth, Ted was equally greatly concerned about his wife. "What about Frances?" he asked, very nervously.

"I must admit that she has had a very difficult time, but she has come through it well and she is going to be fine, too," the doctor reassured him. "That said, her body has suffered some damage and I'm not sure it would be wise for you two to try for any more children."

"Don't worry about that," said a very relieved Ted. "This baby and Frances complete my life and

I'm not going to put either of them in any sort of danger ever again."

Having thanked Doctor Lawrence and escorted him to the door, Ted then went through to the bedroom to see his wife and to meet his newborn son.

"We haven't discussed names at all, but I think I know what you would like to call him," Frances told her husband as he gazed lovingly at the child. "I think you are looking at William Charles Robin."

Ted smiled broadly as he had indeed secretly thought that he would like to name the baby after his two brothers if it was a boy, so he was absolutely delighted to learn that Frances had thought along the same lines.

"Yes, please. If you are content with that, then that is exactly what I would like our little boy to be called," Ted said. "But — and again only if it is okay with you — I really would like it if we can just call him Billy."

"Of course. Billy it is, then," Frances confirmed happily, but then teasingly chastised her husband. "There is one big problem though. The poor child has nowhere to sleep because you have done nothing about a crib for him!"

As Billy Robin was a couple of months early and so a very small baby, Ted was able to create a makeshift bed for him using a shoe-box. He then busied himself over the next few evenings, using his joinery skills to make a crib for his son and over the ensuing few weeks he also made a train set and a model ship, almost identical to those he had made in Radnor several years before.

Chapter 13

Ted's joy was enhanced further still when the time came to christen the baby. He was aware that Frances and Elizabeth had introduced Billy to Nicholas and that Frances often took the baby to their house when Ted was at work. But, as his father had refused to attend Ted's wedding and had barely spoken to him since, he really did not expect Nicholas to attend the christening.

However, when the day came and the Gallen family and friends duly gathered at the Torteval parish church, Ted was pleased to see Dick pulling up in his lorry and not only Ruth and their two children climbing down from the back of it, but also Alfred and Elizabeth ... and Nicholas!

When the ceremony was over and they all filtered out of the church, Nicholas wandered over to Ted and spoke to him for the first time in more than five years.

"Listen, Edwin — we've had our differences in the past and while I cannot forgive or forget them, I am prepared to temper my feelings for the sake of this young man," Nicholas told his son. "After all, with all these foreign incomers to our island, we thoroughbred Guernsey men are becoming a rarity. So, you look after young William and bring him up as God would wish … and make sure he marries a Guernsey girl!"

This was as close as Ted had ever come to hearing his father being humorous and felt himself smiling broadly at this new experience. He thanked Nicholas for putting Billy's wellbeing above their different views and assured him that his grandson would be raised to be a credit to the Robin family.

In much the fashion that Nicholas had indicated, the size and nature of the population of Guernsey was indeed changing significantly. Prior to the Great War, around thirty thousand people lived on the island, most of them indigenous. However, during the ensuing almost fifteen years since the end of the war, large numbers of English people had taken the opportunity to move to the island as the economic situation in their own country worsened.

By the mid-1930s, Guernsey's population had swelled to around forty thousand, with only around half of those being families who had lived there for many generations and the other half being incoming settlers.

As young Billy progressed through his early years, Ted absolutely doted on his son and spent considerable amounts of time playing with the boy, just as Uncle Alf had done with him when he was a lad.

To Frances' slight concern, Ted even insisted on taking Billy with him in the lorry for an hour or two each day as he called at various vineries around the island. The only downside of this for Ted was when the time came for the boy to start at La Chaumière Infants' School, as it did mean that he missed his son's company very much.

Ted was also determined that his son would not have to earn a living through manual labour, in the way that he had done, and so he devoted a lot of time to helping the boy to read and write well and to be good at arithmetic. Billy duly excelled in his early years at school.

The next major development in Ted's life came one Saturday evening in 1938, when he was enjoying a pint in The Beehive with Alfred, and his uncle disclosed to him some exciting news of his own.

"Listen, Ted — I have always envied you going off to America and experiencing a bit of life elsewhere and yet here I am in my late sixties and I have never left this island, so I've decided it's time to do something about it," he said. "I'd be grateful if you would look after my house and shop while I'm away. You don't need to run the shop or anything like that, as it can stay shut for a few weeks. I just want you to keep an eye on my property and make sure that all is well."

Ted was slightly concerned about this sudden addition to his own responsibilities and also about losing his uncle and good friend, even if it was to be for a relatively short period of time. He asked Alfred where he was planning to go.

"Well, I think I'm a bit too long in the tooth to go off to America like you did, but I reckon I might base myself in London and then just visit a few different places around England for a few weeks," he replied.

And so, a few days later, Ted drove Alfred to the harbour in his lorry and waved him off as the ferry set sail for England. Frances aired and dusted Alfred's house once a week, while Ted gave the shop windows and house windows a good wash, but otherwise it transpired that the responsibility of looking after his uncle's property would not impinge too much on their life.

About a month passed and Ted was beginning to wonder how much longer Alfred might be away, when he received a letter from his uncle advising that he was living very happily in a small hotel in London and that he had decided to stay there indefinitely.

The letter went on to ask Ted to sell the furniture in Alf's house and to send the proceeds from that to him as soon as possible. Ted duly did so and then did not hear from his uncle again. The house and shop consequently stood empty and unused and, as more and more weeks rolled by, Ted and Frances became less inclined to clean and maintain the property as they had been doing when they thought Alf's absence would be for only a few weeks.

Ted, Frances and Billy continued to live their simple but happy life. This was the mid to late 1930s, after all, and nobody on the island had a television and only the affluent could afford a radio. They cultivated a section of the field behind their cottage to create a good-sized vegetable patch, planted apple trees and raspberry canes and also built a chicken coup to be able to have their own eggs (and occasionally a roast chicken).

Ted would set off on his bicycle six mornings a week and ride to the depot to collect his lorry, then spend the day collecting boxes of fruit and flowers from vineries around the island and delivering them to the harbour for export to England.

For the first couple of years, Frances would walk Billy to and from La Chaumière Infants School, only half a mile from their home. Then it was to and from Amherst Junior School, which was a mile in the opposite direction. Between these walks, she would spend her time cooking, cleaning the house and tending to their crops and poultry.

Then, each evening after dinner, Ted would help Billy with his reading, writing and arithmetic, although there would always be time before the lad went to bed for a kick-about with a football in the field.

On Sundays, the family would go to Torteval church in the morning, then spend the afternoon either on the beach with Dick and Ruth and their children or else visiting the Gallen family. Then, on Sunday evenings, they would attend St Stephen's church with Nicholas and Elizabeth: Ted's truce with his father seemed to be holding well.

However, while life was ticking along very nicely for most people in Guernsey, Ted became acutely aware of the worrying developments in Europe, so he ensured that he read the Guernsey Press every day. Fears were growing that history would repeat itself with another major war, as Germany's leader, Adolf Hitler, was building up his country's military might and thereby causing great concern among many other European nations.

That concern was shared by many people in Guernsey, where it had never been forgotten that so many of the island's young men had been killed in Northern France during the 1914-18 war. More than twenty years later, the island was still affected by that devastating loss and Ted was not alone in the view that Guernsey might again be asked to surrender the lives of many of its young people to the ravages of war.

In September 1939, the dreadful news came through that Germany had invaded Poland and the British Government immediately declared war on Germany. In the ensuing months, Allied forces did not fare well as the overwhelming strength of the German army again enabled it to advance swiftly through Holland and Belgium and into France.

The residents of Guernsey were again faced with the prospect of invasion by enemy forces, some twenty-five years after they had last been threatened. Yet again, hugely difficult decisions would need to be taken, but this time not just about the island's dairy herd.

Chapter 14

In June 1940, it became clear that a German invasion was indeed imminent and the Guernsey authorities decided to offer evacuation to the island's inhabitants. A small fleet of suitable vessels was organised and arrangements were made with the councils of various towns in the north of England to receive Guernsey evacuees.

A good number of Guernsey parents decided to grasp the opportunity to take their children to the relative safety of Lancashire and Yorkshire. Frances Robin was also very keen that she and Ted and Billy should take the chance to escape German occupation, but was taken aback when her husband said he was having none of it.

"You can go if you want, but I have been called a coward for deserting my island once before and that is not going to happen again," he told her sternly. "I will stay here and look after my parents, but I do accept that you need to take Billy to a safer place."

Frances could see that there was no point in arguing with Ted, but she hated the thought of being apart from him for what might be a considerable period of time. She also hated the thought of being separated from their son, but desperately wanted to ensure that the boy came to no harm at the hands of enemy forces.

Frances resolved that she would remain at Ted's side in Guernsey, but the couple agreed that they did not want their son exposed to whatever the German forces might inflict on the islanders, so they made the desperately difficult decision that Billy should join one of the evacuation parties.

A teacher at Amherst School would be taking charge of a batch of the school's children who were travelling to England and whose parents had decided to stay in Guernsey. A few days later, Ted and Frances stood, distraught, on the quayside at St Peter Port harbour as they waved farewell to their only child, not knowing where he would end up or how long it might be before they would see him again.

In the space of two days, a total of twenty thousand men, women and children made the voyage across the English Channel from Guernsey to Weymouth, of whom there were around five thousand children whose parents had elected to remain in their island home. Some possessed only the clothes they were wearing, while others had a small suitcase containing, perhaps, a change of clothes or a small toy or memento of home.

On the scheduled third day of evacuation, the German Air Force bombed St Peter Port harbour and made it impossible for any more people to get away. Then, on 30th June 1940, German troops landed on Guernsey and began the occupation of the island that would keep many parents and children apart for a full five years.

When the boats that had escaped Guernsey arrived in Weymouth harbour, the evacuees were loaded onto trains right alongside the quayside and transported to places such as Bradford, Bury, Leeds, Manchester, Oldham, Stockport, Wigan and York, where Town Council officials and volunteers were there to greet them.

They were taken to public buildings, such as town halls and dance halls, which had been transformed into Evacuee Reception Centres, where they were greeted by row upon row of camp beds — their homes for up to four weeks or so while host families were found to take them in.

Billy was only nine-years old and although very sad to be parted from his loving parents, he was treating the whole experience as something of an exciting adventure, particularly as he was accompanied by his best friend, Ron Martel.

While most of the children disembarked from trains in northern England, a small contingent continued up to Glasgow. It transpired that one of the schoolteachers accompanying the evacuees was from Glasgow and was in touch with a church there that wanted to assist. Unsure how or why they had been selected to be part of the group heading to Scotland, Billy and Ron were not particularly bothered and were just pleased that they were not being separated.

On arrival in Glasgow, the group was taken to a church hall, remaining there for a couple of weeks. This was not only where they ate and slept, but also where they had their school lessons. The two boys were able to go across the road to play football in a large park for a couple of hours every day though, and overall, they found the whole experience to be quite fun.

One day though, Billy was taken aside by the teacher, who told him that it had been discovered that he had an uncle living in the south of England and that he was going to be sent to live with him. Initially, Billy was very disappointed that he and Ron were going to separated, but then he soon became quite excited at the prospect of seeing Uncle Alf again.

Even though Alfred was Billy's great uncle and getting on a bit in years, he had often joined in when Ted and Billy were kicking a football around in the field and Billy had fond memories of the pranks that Uncle Alf used to play on him and the treats that he used to give him.

So, after bidding a tearful farewell to Ron, Billy began to look forward to the start of yet another adventure as he was taken to Glasgow railway station and put on a train to London. However, on arrival at Waterloo station, he was met by a very different Uncle Alf from the jovial old man that he remembered living next door in Guernsey.

With hardly a word of greeting from his great uncle, Billy was frog-marched across the platform by Alfred and bundled into the carriage of another train, which took them to a town called Sutton on the outskirts of Greater London. Alfred now lived in a small flat above a chip shop and this was to become Billy's home for the next five years.

On the train journey to Sutton, Billy noticed that Uncle Alf was swigging regularly from a hip-flask and moaning to himself that the last thing he needed in his life was the responsibility of looking after a small boy.

"You needn't think I'm going to wet-nurse you, like your parents did," Alf snapped at Billy. "You can learn to stand on your own two feet and if you keep out of my way, then we should get along just fine."

This pronouncement heralded the start of an unhappy and lonely five years for Billy. Not only was his great uncle an alcoholic, but Alfred was also prone to dishing out corporal punishment for the smallest misdemeanour and occasionally, for no reason at all.

Billy also found it difficult to integrate with the other children at his school in Sutton, as to them he was an outsider with a different accent to everybody else and they teased him and refused to befriend him or let him join in their games.

Billy's solution to all this unhappiness was to throw himself into his studies. As well as excelling in the classroom, he also spent a lot of time kicking a football around or throwing a tennis ball against a wall and all of that practice resulted in him becoming an important player in the school's football and cricket teams.

Billy also managed to get a job doing a paper-round each morning before school and his wages enabled him to pay the train fare each weekend to travel into London to visit libraries and museums. All of this complied with Uncle Alf's demand for Billy to keep out of his way, as when Billy returned to the flat each evening, Alf was already across the road in the local public house, So the two of them did not see each other too often throughout the five years.

One of the events that Billy witnessed during his first few months in Sutton in 1940 was the Battle of Britain, with dog-fights raging in the skies above southern England, and he watched as British and German aircraft chased, dodged and fired at each other.

As he lacked the parental control to keep him safely under shelter during and immediately after the air raids on London during the war years, and also because of his early morning paper-round, Billy was often among the first on the scene where bombs had fallen or pieces of damaged aircraft had landed. He soon became a scavenger of shrapnel, spent bullet cartridges and other items, which he was able to sell at school. This helped him to pay for the train fares to and from central London and the entrance fees to get into the museums and libraries there.

Chapter 15

Back in Guernsey, the occupation of the island saw Ted involved in further fall-outs with Nicholas and finally one that was to shatter the relationship between father and son irreparably.

When the German forces had arrived on the island, they were pleased to discover that hundreds of homes had been abandoned by the people who had fled to England and the senior officers set about commandeering these houses in which to billet their troops.

It wasn't too long before the Germans found that Alfred Robin's house was empty and they were even more pleased to find that within his shop were a dozen or so bicycles, all of which they also promptly commandeered.

Four young German soldiers were assigned to live in Alfred's house, much to Nicholas's outrage and his anger was to spill over even more when a German officer entered his workshop on the day that they moved in.

Although nearing his eightieth year, Nicholas still did a couple of hours' work in his joinery shop each day and the sign remained above the door. On discovering that Alfred's house contained no furniture and noticing the sign on Nicholas's workshop, the German officer instructed him to make some beds and cabinets for the German soldiers who would be living in his brother's house.

Nicholas refused point-blank and shouted at the German officer to get out of his workshop and never return. However, the officer threatened that unless Nicholas complied with the order within one week, he would be put in prison.

The old man was adamant that he would rather rot in jail than help the Germans in any way, so it was a very distressed Elizabeth who dashed next door to report this development to their son.

Ted was shocked that the Germans should even consider treating an old man in such fashion, even if it was his very belligerent father. He went to the offices of the German High Command, where he advised that he too was a master joiner and that he would make the furniture for them if they promised not to put his father in prison.

Ted returned to his parents' house and told them that the Germans had agreed to let him make the furniture for the soldiers in Alf's house and therefore Nicholas would not have to go to prison. However, his father was appalled to learn what his son had done and ranted that he was ashamed that any of his family would collaborate with the enemy.

"It is not collaboration, as I am not assisting the German war effort," Ted tried to reason with his father. "I am simply giving four young men something more comfortable to sleep on than the floor and that is hardly going to help Hitler to win the war."

Nicholas remained outwardly unhappy: although secretly gratified that his son still thought enough of him to want to keep him out of prison, this incident served only to put a renewed strain on their relationship.

The German forces also commandeered Dick's lorries and drivers to transport concrete and other building materials, as they built huge watch-towers and bunkers around the coastline of the island, but they did at least pay Dick a small sum of money for doing so.

This caused Nicholas to again complain that Dick and Ted were collaborating with the enemy. Ted tried to point out to him that as it was impossible to export local produce to England, they might as well agree to drive the lorries for the Germans as it meant that they were getting paid and so had money to buy food for their families.

However, one cargo that Ted did refuse to transport in his lorry were the slave labourers who had been brought from Eastern Europe to build the watch-towers and bunkers. These poor souls were accommodated in rat-infested camps, fed very meagre rations and given only a little water to drink each day.

Rather than risk letting the Germans become aware of Ted's strong objection to the treatment of the slave labourers though, Dick always ensured that Ted never carried any of the 'human loads' and always put him on the trips where his lorry contained only building materials.

The four young German soldiers who lived in Alfred's house tended to keep pretty much to themselves, although Ted and Frances saw no harm in saying 'Good Morning' or other appropriate greetings to them, while praying that Nicholas did not hear them doing so.

Both the Guernsey people and their German occupiers managed to eat and drink fairly well during the first three years or so of the occupation of the island and the soldiers tended not to encroach on the civilians' food supply sources.

This was because regular shipments arrived from nearby France, so the German soldiers had a ready supply of food and other provisions. Meanwhile, with the export of locally grown and reared produce rendered impossible, the Guernsey people had their own ready supply of vegetables, milk, beef, fish and poultry.

However, this situation was to change dramatically in the last two years of Guernsey's occupation. Towards the end of 1943 and into early

1944, the Allies began to take the upper hand in the war and Germany suffered significant setbacks in North Africa, Russia and Italy.

This, in turn, meant that German resources in France were redeployed to areas where they could mount a better defence of their own country's borders and this resulted in the cessation of supply ships sailing across to the Channel Islands. The occupying forces therefore grew hungry and began to help themselves to the crops and livestock belonging to the local population.

Ted and Frances had kept chickens in the field behind their cottage and they began to notice their daily harvest of eggs diminishing. Frances also worked the area of the field given over to growing vegetables and fruit, but again items of this produce were going missing.

She kept a sharp lookout through her kitchen window and one day when Ted came home for work, Frances told him that she had seen one of the German soldiers stealing some of their eggs. Ted immediately stormed next door to Alfred's house and confronted the four young soldiers, who immediately confessed that they had taken eggs and fruit and vegetables because they were so hungry.

"I understand that you are very hungry, but you should not resort to stealing," Ted chided them. "We would be quite happy to share our food with you, but certainly not if you show us so little respect."

The German soldiers seemed to be full of remorse and apologised to Ted, who then astonished them by inviting them to join him and Frances for dinner the following evening. They readily accepted and Ted went out to the field, wrung the neck of one of their chickens, plucked it and asked Frances to prepare it for dinner the next day.

Nicholas was very concerned when he saw four German soldiers entering his son's cottage the following evening, so he went to investigate. Needless to say, he was absolutely aghast when he went inside to see Ted, Frances and the four soldiers sitting around the dining table with plates of roast chicken, potatoes and vegetables and the group listening as Ted said grace.

"For God's sake, it's bad enough that I see you speaking to these people, but to share your food with them is a disgusting show of fraternisation!" Nicholas raged. "You have brought shame on me before, but I will never be able to hold my head up in the community when they all discover that my son is a collaborator!"

While his father's reaction came as little surprise to Ted, he hoped that by explaining the personal and religious reasons behind his actions, Nicholas might at least understand them.

"These young men find themselves in a strange country because of a war that was none of their making and I know just how that feels," Ted told him. "They are only a few years older than my own son and I would not be doing my Christian duty if I did not share some of my food with them, when it is clear that they are starving."

Nicholas had learned from past encounters that it was pointless to continue arguing with his son, but he left Ted in no doubt that the truce between them had now ceased and that he was disowning his son for a second and final time.

The civilised arrangement between Ted and his German neighbours was not replicated across the island and it became standard practice for many of the other German soldiers to simply help themselves to any available food. This meant that by the early months of 1945, virtually all the cows, pigs, goats and rabbits on the island had been slaughtered and the crops of vegetables and fruit had also been exhausted.

The local population had to resort to making nettle soup and seaweed bread, while even seagulls and rats became targets for shots from German guns as the troops tried to get their hands on anything resembling food.

Some islanders had small fishing boats and had been allowed to venture a few hundred yards off-shore in search of fish and shellfish, although to go beyond the limit laid down by the Germans would have incurred being fired on by the huge guns sited around the island's coastline. Again though, it became standard practice for any local fishing boat returning to shore to be met by German soldiers who would confiscate some or all of their catch.

One thing that greatly distressed Ted and most other islanders was that the slave workers were even worse off during this time than the Guernsey people or their occupiers. While some of them dared to try to throw pieces of their seaweed-bread over the barbed-wire fences of the compounds in which the slave workers were kept, many of these poor souls were to die from starvation.

Those early months of 1945 also saw bitterly cold winter conditions which, combined with their own poor diet, also brought dire consequences for some of the elderly and infirm Guernsey residents. Not only did they have very little to eat, they were also often unable to light their fires because the German soldiers were taking all available wood for their own fires.

Nicholas fell gravely ill and despite Elizabeth and Frances caring for him day and night for some weeks, he finally died on 27th January 1945, ironically on his grandson Billy's sixteenth birthday. Nicholas and Ted had not spoken to each other in more than a year and Nicholas refused Elizabeth's plea to let their son sit by his bedside in his final days. Still, Ted was very upset when his father passed away.

Tragically, his grief was to be all the more acute only a month later, when Elizabeth also succumbed to the freezing cold and poor diet and she, too, passed away. Ted's parents had both died only a couple of months before the island was to be liberated and much better times lay ahead.

While Nicholas had been a difficult man to live with, he and Elizabeth had been together for more than fifty years: Ted and Frances came to believe that Elizabeth had died as much from a broken heart as from her advanced years and ailing health.

Chapter 16

On 1st May 1945, as it seemed that both the local community and the German soldiers on Guernsey would suffer the same fate as the slave workers and some of the elderly islanders, news came through that Adolf Hitler had committed suicide in a bunker in Berlin and the Allies were making the final push to victory.

Massive Allied bombing of German cities — in particular, Dresden, being almost completely destroyed — soon brought all resistance to an end and on 8th May, the German High Command finally succumbed to demands for full and unconditional surrender.

The German troops in Guernsey duly laid down their arms and many of them were then subjected to severe taunting and in some cases, even beatings from some of the triumphant islanders. Indeed, they were therefore almost as relieved as the local residents when British troops arrived at St Peter Port harbour on 9th May and proceeded to take control of the island.

German soldiers were shipped off the island to prisoner-of-war camps in the UK or France over the next few weeks, while thousands of evacuees sailed home to Guernsey. However, many of the evacuated families had made new lives for themselves in the towns of northern England and so elected to stay there, instead.

Ships sailed to Guernsey regularly, bringing food parcels, sacks of grain and young animals, as every effort was made to return the island to some sort of normality after five years of occupation and, in the last year or so, several months of near starvation.

One lovely summer's morning in late June, as they stood on the quayside at St Peter Port harbour waiting for the ferry to dock, Ted and Frances were about to see a considerable difference in the small boy they had waved off from the same spot some five years earlier. Back then they had shared hugs and tears with a small, nine-year-old boy in short trousers and a school cap, so they hardly recognised the gangly youth walking towards them wearing flannels and a cricket sweater.

Billy also noticed how much his parents had changed since he last saw them: both were much thinner and his father's hair had turned grey. He extended an arm to shake hands with his father, but then flinched when his mother tried to embrace him. Billy had not experienced any similar affection in all the time that he had lived with Uncle Alfred, so it felt really quite strange and almost embarrassing to have someone trying to hug him.

The three of them climbed into Ted's lorry and as they drove up the hill from St Peter Port and along the road to their cottage, Ted broke the news to Billy that Nicholas and Elizabeth had both perished in the deprived times that the island had faced, towards the end of the war. They resolved that they would visit the family grave in St Stephen's churchyard after the service the following Sunday, so that Billy could pay his respects to his grandparents.

Once indoors and while Frances prepared them a meal, Billy told his parents about his time living with Uncle Alf and how the old man had treated him and occasionally beaten him. Ted was absolutely aghast to learn that his uncle had been so poor in his stewardship of their son and found himself filled with quite un-Christian thoughts about what he might do to Alfred if and when he ever saw him again.

"Don't worry. It worked out okay really, because Uncle Alf spent most of his time across the road in the pub," Billy told his parents. "He was in bed when I left in the mornings and I was in bed when he came home at night, so we really didn't see much of each other at all."

Aside from their despair on hearing about Alfred, Ted and Frances were very pleased to learn that their son had excelled academically and had gained a scholarship to the Grammar School in Sutton. He had been in the top two or three in the class in every subject and had also represented his school in cricket, football and athletics. A few days later, they received a letter from the island's education department to advise that Billy was to attend the Grammar School in Guernsey (or the Intermediate School, as it was known then).

Sutton Council wrote to Ted a few weeks after Billy's return to Guernsey, to advise that Alfred had died from an alcohol-related illness and that his body was to be repatriated to Guernsey for burial. While making the arrangements for the funeral and then attending it, Ted felt a little guilty that he experienced very little sorrow at his uncle's passing, but he simply could not forgive Alf for his neglect of Billy at such a difficult time in the young boy's life.

As the sole beneficiary of the wills of both Nicholas and Alfred, Ted was able to sell both of their properties. Many English people were choosing to move to Guernsey in order to try to escape the even more severe post-war austerity that was prevailing in their own country.

The income from the sale of the two houses, together with their decision to remain in their modest little cottage rather than spend any of it on a larger property, meant that Ted and Frances were relatively wealthy at a time of rationing and sacrifice for many of their fellow islanders.

In the autumn of 1945, an advertisement appeared on the front page of the Guernsey Press, which brought back memories and also a wry smile to Ted's face.

Virtually all of the island's livestock had been slaughtered, as both its community and the occupying soldiers looked for every available source of food. While goats, sheep and poultry could be sent over from the UK, the authorities recalled that examples of Guernsey's unique breed of cattle were living in America and resolved to recall some of them to the island. An advertisement was placed in the Guernsey Press.

"Young men required to travel to America to escort Guernsey cattle back to the island. Anyone interested should contact the Guernsey Agriculture Council for further details."

Ted smiled as he recalled a similar advertisement more than thirty years earlier, but he swiftly resolved that he was neither young enough, nor even the slightest bit inclined, to make that particular journey once again!

Post-Script

Ted Robin died in 1958, two years after seeing his son Billy get married and one year after his first grandchild was born. Frances kept her promise to her husband that she would not reveal to anyone the details of his time in America and she died in 1974 with that secret still intact.

It was only some years later, when Billy grew interested in researching his family history, that his investigations uncovered his father's Ellis Island immigration record and, in the Radnor Church register, the marriage of Ted and Edith.

Billy decided to tell his own son about Ted's American adventure and when Billy died in 2019, Neil Robin then felt that the story deserved to be shared with a wider audience.